W9-CBT-274

# In the Valley

# In the Valley

*Stories and a Novella Based on* **Serena**

**Ron Rash**

**Doubleday**

*New York*

Several pieces first appeared in the following publications: "Neighbors" in
*Epoch* (2018) and *Best American Mystery Stories 2019;* "When All the Stars
Fall" in *Southword* (2019); "Sad Man in the Sky" in *Bitter Southerner* (2019);
"L'homme Blessé" in *Ploughshares* (2018); "The Baptism" in *Southern Review*
(2017) and *Best American Short Stories 2018;* "Flight" in *Washington Square
Review* (2020); "Last Bridge Burned" in *The Masters Review* (2018); and "The
Belt" in *South Carolina Review* (2018).

Book design by Maria Carella
Jacket image: *Stump,* 2000, color woodcut (detail) © Neil Welliver,
courtesy of the Alexandre Gallery
Photo credit: Ackland Art Museum,
The University of North Carolina at Chapel Hill/Art Resource, NY
Jacket design by Emily Mahon

Library of Congress Cataloging-in-Publication Data
Names: Rash, Ron, 1953—author.
Title: In the valley : stories and a novella based on Serena / Ron Rash.
Description: First edition. | New York : Doubleday, [2020]
Identifiers: LCCN 2019058231 | ISBN 9780385544290 (hardcover) |
ISBN 9780385544306 (ebook)
Classification: LCC PS3568.A698 A6 2020 | DDC 813/.54—dc23
LC record available at https://lccn.loc.gov/2019058231IP

1 3 5 5 7 9 10 8 6 4 2

First Edition

*For Collins Lee Rash*

And I do not mean the faith which flees the
world, but the one that endures the world and
that loves and remains true to the world in
spite of all the suffering which it contains for us.

# Contents

# In the Valley

# Neighbors

They came at dawn, ground crackling beneath the trample of hooves, amid it the sound of chickens flapping and squawking. Then voices, one among them shouting to dismount. The corn shucks rasped as Rebecca rose, quickly tugging her wool overcoat tight against her gown. She waked the children. As they rubbed questioning eyes, Rebecca whispered for them to get under the bed and be absolutely still. Hannah's chin quivered but she nodded. Ezra, three years older, took his sister's hand as they raised themselves off the mattress. He helped Hannah underneath and followed.

A pounding on the door began as Rebecca gathered the salt pouch from the larder, the box of matches off the fireboard. She considered lifting the loose plank beneath the table and placing what filled her hands inside the clay crock, but the pounding was so fierce now that the door latch looked ready to splinter. Rebecca shoved the salt and matches beneath the bed too, whispered a last plea for the children to be quiet. She waited a few moments, some wisp of hope that the men might simply take the chickens and the ham in the barn and leave. But the man at the door shouted that they'd burn out those inside if the door didn't open.

Rebecca knew they would, that these men had done worse things in Shelton Laurel. Just months ago, they'd whipped Sallie Moore until blood soaked her back, roped Martha White to a tree and beat her. Barns had been burned, wells fouled with slaughtered animals. *There's nary a meanness left for them rebels to do to us,* Ginny Lunsford had claimed, but she'd been proved wrong the next day when eleven men and a thirteen-year-old boy were marched west a mile on the Knoxville pike, lined up, and shot.

Rebecca lifted the latch. As she pushed the door open, boot steps clattered off the porch. A low swirling fog made the horses mere gray shapes, those mounted upon them adrift, like revenants. Rebecca stepped far enough out to show her empty hands. A rein shook and a horse moved forward, its rider a man whose age lay hidden behind a thick brown beard. He alone wore an actual uniform, though his butternut jacket lacked two buttons, his officer's hat stained and slouched. He raised a hand, but before tipping his hat he caught himself, set the hand on the saddle pommel. The man asked if anyone else was inside.

Rebecca hesitated.

"I'm Colonel Allen, of the North Carolina 64th regiment," he said. "You've heard of us, of me."

"Yes."

"Then you know you'll rue any lie you tell me."

"My chaps," Rebecca said. "They're but seven and four."

"Anyone else?"

"No."

"Bring them out here," Colonel Allen said, and turned to a tall man behind him.

Rebecca went inside, kneeled by the bed, and helped the children to their feet. Hannah whimpered, Ezra's eyes wide with fear.

"Will they kill us, Mother?" Ezra asked.

"No," Rebecca answered, her hands huddling them onto the porch. "But we must do what is asked."

They stood beside the cord of wood Brice Fothergill had cut for them in October, accepting nothing for his labor. Rebecca took off the overcoat and covered the children. After all of the men had tethered their horses, Colonel Allen and the sergeant stood in front of the porch as the other men gathered behind them. The chickens had calmed and several clucked and pecked nearby.

"Come a little closer, chickees," one of the soldiers said, "and I'll give ye neck a nice stretch."

Hannah started to cry. Rebecca stroked the child's flaxen hair as she whispered for her to hush.

"Them young ones look stout for their ages," the sergeant said. "Must be eating well."

"A nit makes a louse," a soldier wearing a black eye patch said, and another man loudly agreed.

Allen raised a hand and the men grew quiet.

"Your man," he asked, "where is he?"

"Likely hiding up on the ridge," the sergeant said, "waiting to take a shot at us once we're headed back. That's their way up here, ain't it?"

"Yes, Sergeant," Allen said, staring at Rebecca as he spoke. "They'll not face us like soldiers. They leave their women and children behind to do that."

"I've got no man," Rebecca said.

"What about them children," the sergeant scoffed. "They just sprout out of the ground like toadstools?"

"My husband's dead."

"Dead," Allen said skeptically. "How long has he been dead?"

"She's lying," the sergeant said when she hesitated. "Him and some of his bluebelly neighbors is probably beading us right now."

"Aaron's been dead two years," Rebecca said.

The sun had climbed the ridge now, and yellow light settled on the yard and cabin. The fog began unknitting into loose gray strands and all could be seen—the outhouse and spring, the barn where a ham wrapped in cheesecloth hung from a rafter, stored above it hay for the calf her closest neighbor, Ira Wilkey, would bring once it was weaned. Unlike many in Shelton Laurel, Ira had enough land to hide his livestock, so offered the calf for a quilt Rebecca made from what clothing Aaron left behind. We'll not make it through these times if we don't look after each other, Ira answered when she protested the trade was unfair to him.

The sergeant stepped to the side of the cabin, his eyes sweeping the clearing.

"I don't see no grave."

"Aaron ain't buried here," Rebecca said.

"No?" Allen said. "Where then?"

"In Asheville."

"Which cemetery in Asheville?" the sergeant asked.

"I can't remember its name," Rebecca said.

"I told you what we do to liars," Allen said.

"I argue he's close by, sir," the sergeant said. "He could be hiding in the barn."

"Take two men and go look, Corporal," Allen said to the man with the eye patch.

"Where's your pa, boy?" the sergeant asked.

Behind them now, Rebecca pulled the overcoat tighter around the children.

"All he knows is his daddy's dead."

"That right, son?" Allen asked. "Your pa's dead?"

"Tell him your daddy's dead," Rebecca said.

"Yes, sir," Ezra said softly.

"Where's he buried, boy?" the sergeant asked.

"He don't know none of that," Rebecca said.

"That right, son?" Allen asked.

"Yes, sir."

"Yes, sir, what? You know or you don't know?"

Ezra looked at the ground.

"I don't know," he whispered.

"I can likely guess some places," Allen said to his sergeant. "Can't you?"

"Antietam or Gettysburg maybe."

"I'd say more likely Tennessee, since they head west to join. Shiloh or Stones River, there or maybe Donaldson."

At the last word Rebecca's right hand clutched Hannah's shoulder so hard the child gave a sharp cry.

"So it was Donaldson," the sergeant said.

Rebecca didn't respond.

"My first cousin was killed at Donaldson," Allen said. "A good man with children no older than those you got your hands on."

"I had a friend killed there," the sergeant added. "Grapeshot ripped his legs off."

The two men said nothing more, appearing to expect some response. The corporal and the two men came out of the barn.

"Ain't no one hiding in there," the corporal said, "but there's a ham curing and it's enough to give some bully soldiers a full feeding."

One of the men whooped and slapped a palm twice against his belly.

"What else is in the barn?" Allen asked.

"No livestock," the corporal said, "but enough hay to make a pretty fire."

The only sound was the snort of a horse as Rebecca and the men waited for Colonel Allen to give his orders. *Soldiers.* That was what the corporal claimed them to be. Rebecca thought of the men sketched in the newspapers her father-in-law had brought with Aaron's letters in the war's first months. Those soldiers wore plumed hats and buttoned jackets, sabers and sashes strapped on their waists. They looked heroic and Rebecca knew that many, like Aaron, had been. Some of these men before her were surely heroic at one time too, but now their ill-matched clothing offered no sign of allegiance except to their own thievery.

"Bost," Allen said to a man who wore a frock coat Rebecca recognized, "you and Murdock and Etheridge gather what chickens you can."

Several men shouted encouragement as Bost dove for the closest chicken. White feathers slapped his face until he pinned the bird firmly to the ground.

"Kill it now?" Bost panted, his scratched face looking up at the colonel.

"No, we'll take them with us."

A second man retrieved a burlap sack and the squawking chicken was shoved inside. Bost knotted the sack and tied it to a saddle as the other two men began their own chases.

"Take a man and get that ham, Corporal," Allen said. "Sergeant, go inside. Look around good. You know how they hide things."

"Nothing inside is worth your while," Rebecca said. "There's a root cellar behind the barn. It's partial hid by old board planks. Near all what food we have is there." She met Allen's eyes, saw that, like Aaron's had been, there were gold flecks within the brown. "These chaps are cold. Just let me and them go inside, and you take everything else."

"She must be hiding something real good," the sergeant said. "It's yankee money or clothes that boy there can't fill. Maybe the son of a bitch himself is hiding under the bed."

"Go see then," Allen said, and turned to Rebecca. "You and your children come on out here."

"Let me get their shoes first," Rebecca said, but Allen shook his head.

Rebecca settled Hannah on her hip and took Ezra's hand. They went down the porch's one step and into the yard. As Allen gave more orders, Rebecca glanced furtively toward the ridge, looking for a bright wink of sun on metal, then looked farther down the valley. Smoke rose from Ira Wilkey's farm and, beyond it, Brice and Anna Fothergill's home, which meant the Confederates had come in the night unseen. Hannah began whimpering again, but Ezra stood silent, his hands balled into fists. *Don't*, she whispered, and used her free hand to open his.

She should have burned the letters, as she had done with the newspapers her father-in-law had brought. But there were only five because Aaron died early in the war, so early her father-in-law had been able to travel the eighteen miles from Asheville in broad daylight, this before bush-whackers as well as Colonel Allen and his men made any stranger in Shelton Laurel a suspected spy or thief, thus shot on sight. *I will return with a wagon to take you and the children back to live with me.* That was her father-in-law's promise when he'd brought the last letter, which contained a brass button taken from Aaron's field jacket. *My hope is that this button might offer some remembrance,* Aaron's com-mander had written.

But her father-in-law had not come again, with or with-out a wagon, and Rebecca had wondered if it was suspicion of her allegiance, not fear, that had kept him away.

"Put a match to the barn?" the corporal asked when he'd returned with the ham.

"We'll feed our horses first," Allen said, as men returned with potatoes and apples from the root cellar, what chick-ens had been caught.

The two privates came out of the cabin, one holding the salt pouch and matches. The sergeant followed, in his hands the crock.

"It's near all letters, except for this," the sergeant said. He cradled the container with his elbow as he reached inside and removed a button with CSA stamped into the brass.

He handed it to Allen, who examined the button a moment before putting it in his jacket pocket.

"You know it was took off one of our own, probably killed up here by some coward sniping from behind a tree."

"What do the letters say?" Allen asked.

"You know I never had any school learning, Colonel."

Rebecca glanced toward the ridge, then the closer woods before she spoke.

"Please," she said softly.

Colonel Allen took the crock and sat on the porch step. He lifted the lid, took out a letter, and began to read. As he did so, Rebecca remembered the night Aaron had packed the travel trunk with clothing but also his briar pipe, pocket watch, and penknife, the tintype taken on their wedding day. She thought of the two shirts and pair of breeches he'd left, cut up for Ira's quilt, and how her fingers lingered on those cloth squares, sometimes pressing one against her cheek.

After he'd read the first letter, Allen read quicker, then merely scanned. Coming to the last, which, unlike the others, had been written on rag paper, he read slowly again, then raised his eyes.

"Why didn't you tell us?" he asked, his voice as perplexed as his eyes.

When Rebecca didn't respond, he refolded the letter carefully and set it back in the container. Colonel Allen placed the lid back on and stood.

"Tell the men to put everything back, Sergeant Reeves."

"Sir?" the sergeant said.

"Free those chickens, and put that ham back too," Allen said, addressing the corporal as well. When the sergeant didn't respond, he added, "That's a direct order."

"Yes, sir," the sergeant said, not alone in watching hungrily as the ham was returned to the barn.

"Mrs. Penland, it is too cold for you and your children to be out here," Allen said. "You must go inside."

He took off his hat and followed them. Colonel Allen set the crock on the fireboard and went out to the porch, first for kindling, then one of the hearth logs Brice Fothergill had cut. Allen took a tin of matches from his pocket and lit the kindling, waved his hat to coax the fire into being.

"You children," he said as he stood. "Come closer and get warm. You too, ma'am."

Rebecca did as he said, placing the children before her. The flames thickened and Hannah and Ezra ceased to shiver. Rebecca took a quilt from the bed and laid it before the fire.

"Lay down there," she told them.

"Their real ages?" Allen asked.

"Seven and ten."

"Yes," he said, looking at them. "I guessed about that. Had my son and daughter lived, they would have soon been their sizes."

Rebecca hesitated, then spoke.

"I know," she said, "about their dying, I mean. It's said you blame people here for it."

"They are to blame. They came at night like cowards and terrorized my wife and sick children. Do you deny that?"

"No," Rebecca said.

The sergeant knocked and opened the door.

"Your orders have been carried out."

Colonel Allen nodded and the door closed.

"The commendation from General Buckner," he said, nodding at the fireboard. "It speaks well of your Aaron as a soldier, and the letters speak equally well of him as husband and father. I regret that I had to peruse them, but it was necessary. I ask your forgiveness for that and for what has occurred today. I, we, will attempt recompense. We have sugar, and if you need more wood cut . . ."

"No," Rebecca said. "I want nothing from you but what you and your men came here to do."

"Your anger at our ill treatment I understand, Mrs. Penland, but had you simply told us what we now know."

"And after you're gone, what do you think will happen if you and your men leave this farm as if you'd never come?"

Colonel Allen's mouth tightened into a grimace. The only sound was the fire's hiss and crackle. Rebecca looked down and saw that Hannah's eyes were already closed. Ezra's too were beginning to droop, though his mouth remained in a defiant pout.

"What would you have us do then?"

"What you came here to do," Rebecca answered, "that and you and your men don't tell anyone about the letters."

He nodded and stepped to the doorway.

"Corporal, go get the ham."

"But, sir, you said . . ."

"I know what I said. Get the men to catch three chickens, no more. You can kill them. We'll eat them when we're out of this godforsaken valley."

"That won't be enough," Rebecca said.

Allen turned.

"Yes, it will."

"No," Rebecca said. "It won't be."

"What more then would you have me do? You have no well to foul."

"The barn, you must burn it."

"I will not do that, Mrs. Penland. Your husband died for our cause. The ham and chickens will be enough. Tell your neighbors we were here only minutes. Say we set the barn afire but did not stay to ensure if it fully caught. But those letters, they *should* be burned. If one of your neighbors were to come upon them . . ."

Colonel Allen stepped out of the door and gave orders to mount.

The clatter of the men and horses leaving did not wake the children. Rebecca went outside, looked down the valley, and saw that smoke yet hovered above the two farms. A skein of smoke, nothing like the billowing plumes that rose a year ago at Brice and Anna's place, last June at Ira's. Everyone in Shelton Laurel would soon know the soldiers had come. They would hear or see them passing on the pike that led back to Marshall. Some of the men might have time to fire a few shots. Then they would come and see if Rebecca and the children were safe.

But they would not arrive for a little while, so Rebecca went inside the cabin. Not wanting to waste a match, she pulled a half-burned piece of kindling from the hearth and walked to the barn. *Nine years,* Rebecca thought, remembering how Ezra was already kicking in her belly when she and Aaron had arrived from Buncombe County. The cabin had been here, but not the barn. Ira had come first to help, then others bringing axes and oxen. In a week the barn had been built. She remembered Aaron's warning the night before he left for Asheville—*Always say Unionist.*

A thick matting of straw lay in an empty stall. Rebecca dropped the kindling and soon flames spilled into the adjoining stalls before laddering up gate posts and beams. Only when flame blossomed in the loft did Rebecca leave the barn. Frost still limned the ground, and that was a blessing. It would keep the fire from spreading.

When she'd returned to the cabin, Rebecca opened the crock and saw Colonel Allen had not put the button back. *Not even his button, not even that,* she thought, as she took out the letters and held them above the flames. Foolish not to have done it before, Rebecca knew, and told herself to open her hand and let them go.

But she couldn't, so Rebecca put them in the container and placed it back in the cubbyhole. She went outside and saw that the barn had crumpled except for the locust beams. The thick smoke that clouded the sky minutes before was now no more, signaling to neighbors that the Confederates were gone.

By the time Ira and Brice arrived, the fire would be no more than a smolder. The two men would kick the ashes, hoping to find a locust beam with only its surface charred. They'd douse the beam with water from the spring and drag it from the rubble. The Ledford and Hampton men would arrive next, and soon after whole families. The Lunsfords and Smiths, then the Moores and the Sheltons. The women would bring food enough to get Rebecca and the children through the winter. Men would bring axes and the surrounding woods would sound like gunshots as the honed metal struck in the November air. All day the women would cook and tend fires. Children would gather kindling, then scuff among ashes for the iron nails that had secured the shingles. Everyone would work until dusk, then return the next day to help more. Ira Wilkey might or might not say *We will get through this together*, but that was understood. They were neighbors.

# When All the Stars Fall

There had been no shade as they built the dock, and though they wore sunscreen, the skin between shirt and ball cap had been burned to the color of brick. Brent and his father rubbed calamine lotion on their necks each night, but the skin remained tender to the touch as if branded. But now it was after five on Friday afternoon and the dock was nearly done, would have been done, Brent knew, if someone other than his father had taken the job. They'd have already packed up their saws and drills, gone up to Mr. Hewitt's house to get their check, and be sipping a beer at Mac's Bar and Grill.

Instead, the old man had checked everything up top and now waded into the water to confirm that every post was meticulously secured. Only then would he and Brent walk the shore to ensure no wood chips or screws littered the ground. *Even if they never notice, it has to be done right,* his father always said. Which was why, despite Brent's protestations, the old man would hand a client a piece of notebook paper with an itemized cost of materials and labor. If the price was agreed on, his father asked for nothing more than a handshake. Several times the job, once begun, took more materials and labor than anticipated. When that happened, he explained the situation but left it up to the owner to decide on additional compensation. Having worked ten years with his father, Brent was no longer surprised at how often those with the most money balked at paying extra. Such customers also searched intently for some flaw on a completed deck or dock. If they were insistent enough, his father dropped the price a few dollars. Not as much as they'd like, but enough to stop their complaining and write the check.

Brent's father waded out of the shallows, the black Maglite held overhead like a torch. He'd rolled his pants above the knees, and in the day's declining light his legs glowed in their paleness. Unlike his muscular arms and shoulders, his legs were thin, each footstep tentative as he waded ashore. Even after a second surgery, the right knee gave way at times, part of the price for countless hours kneeling on wood and concrete.

"Looks good," his father said, so they checked the shoreline and packed the last of their tools into the pickup.

They were glad this job was done. Mr. Hewitt had a reputation as being hard to work for. "A royal pain in the ass," a brick mason had told Brent and his father. Jerry Funderburke, who worked at Lowe's, swore he'd quit the store before going to Hewitt's house again. So Brent and his father had been warned, but since the recession, carpentry work was scarce. Too many days they'd waited at home for the phone to ring, Brent even working part-time at Hardee's to make extra money. He and Leslie had been talking about having a child, yet how could they when the two of them together barely made each month's rent and car loan. But it was Friday, Brent reminded himself. The job was done and they had work for next week already lined up. In a few minutes they would stop at Mac's for a beer before Brent's father dropped him off. If they weren't too tired, maybe he and Leslie could drive to Sylva to rent a movie.

Hewitt was on the lake house's back deck, which was no surprise, because he'd been there often during the week. He'd come down to the dock every day. "I'm just wanting to see how far you got," Mr. Hewitt would say, but his eyes always searched for something more. "You're certain those are the right board length?" he'd ask, or "Will those screws hold securely?" They were questions tinged with accusation. Brent's father answered, "Yes, sir," but after Hewitt left he'd muttered, "That man knows as much about dock building as a cross-eyed cat."

Mr. Hewitt came down the deck steps with a checkbook in his hand.

"I want to look it over first," he said, and they followed him onto the dock, the boards firm beneath their feet. Farther up the lake, a red sun balanced on the hydro dam. A cool breeze swayed the cattails and Brent thought how nice it would be to sit out here with an ice chest of beer as the last Jet Skis or boats went in. All you'd hear was water sloshing softly against the posts.

"It's a pretty view," his father said, looking out at the lake as well.

"Maybe so," Mr. Hewitt said, "but this railing's too high for the dock to be safe for a child."

"You didn't say you wanted it lower," his father answered. "You didn't say a word about children."

"A professional would consider something like that and consult the client, don't you think?"

His father's face burned as if he'd been slapped, except Brent knew a slap would sting less.

"You were out here yesterday when we began putting it up," Brent said. "You should have said something then."

"I wasn't looking that carefully," Mr. Hewitt answered. "I assumed you knew what you were doing. I'll pay you half of what we agreed on."

The breeze that had bent the cattails ceased. The water stilled as if the lake itself now listened. Brent looked at Mr. Hewitt. What did he know about this man, besides that he was wealthy and from some place where you could make enough money to own a vacation home worth half a million dollars.

"It'll take another day," his father finally said, "but we can lower the railing where you want it."

"And listen to more of the racket your saws and drills have made all week?" Mr. Hewitt answered. "I bought this place for the peace and quiet. No, I'll have it redone sometime when I'm away."

"It's not right," Brent's father said. "We've done good honest work for you."

Mr. Hewitt set the checkbook on the railing, took a pen from his shirt pocket, and wrote out the check. He held it out to Brent's father, who stared at the check as if it was smeared with dog shit.

"This is what I'm paying you," Hewitt said.

"You owe us the full amount," Brent said, "and you're going to pay it."

"Look, if you've got a problem, we can take this to court. But you'd better take the check and be on your way, because if my lawyer gets involved you will end up with nothing."

His father took the check.

"We'll call us a lawyer first thing in the morning," Brent's father said when they got in the truck. "There's got to be some that work on Saturday."

"It won't be worth it, Dad," Brent replied, looking out at the lake. "A lawyer will cost more than what Hewitt owes us, even if we won. Like I've been telling you for months, this is exactly why we need to make out real contracts, to protect ourselves."

"There's lawyers that take a case for a percentage," his father said. "You see them on TV all the time."

"Not for this small an amount."

"There might be one around who'd do it that way," his father said, "just for the principle of the thing."

"It doesn't work that way," Brent said, trying not to sound exasperated. "Why don't we skip Mac's this evening? We'll do it next Friday."

"I don't feel much like stopping myself," his father agreed, then as much to himself as to Brent, "I don't understand how anyone can act that way and still sleep at night."

They didn't speak again until the pickup pulled into the driveway. Brent got out and took his lunch container and circular saw from the back, then walked over to the driver's-side door.

"I'll see you Monday, Dad."

"Why don't you and Leslie come to church Sunday?" his father said. "Folks there have been asking about you all. Afterward you could come to the house for lunch. That would tickle your mom. Besides, I've been craving banana pudding and she makes it only for you."

"We'll see," Brent said.

Leslie was already home, but he didn't go straight inside. Instead, Brent put the saw and lunch box beside the shed and sat in a swing the previous renters had put up. He'd quit smoking two years ago, but he wanted one bad right now. *How can anyone act that way?* his father had asked.

Brent had known Ricky Lunsford since first grade. A pale, pudgy boy who carried around an inhaler for his asthma, Ricky had been the kid in elementary school who never got chosen when teams were decided. There had been some teasing, a few times he'd been shoved or tripped, but Ricky never asked a teacher to intervene, and earned a bit of respect for that. He'd retreat to the playground's far corner at recess. In high school Ricky sat alone at lunch. *Just ignore me,* he made clear. *Do that and I'll ask no more of you.*

But one day in the eleventh grade, Brent paused at the table where Ricky sat. You don't need this, Brent said, and took the piece of pizza off Ricky's plate before walking on to where his friends were. Brent did that for two weeks, taking something—pizza, a hamburger, a carton of milk—never a whole plate. Just one thing. Ricky never tried to stop it. He never said a word, just let it happen. By the second week Brent didn't bother to put what he took on his plate. He carried the pilfered food to the nearest trash can and dropped it in.

If a teacher hadn't seen what was happening, how long

would he have done it? Not much longer, Brent wanted to believe, but he'd never know for certain, because one afternoon the principal called Brent's parents. That evening he and his father went to visit the Lunsfords. Brent had never seen where Ricky lived. It was a trailer with rust bleeding down the dented tin, concrete blocks rising irregularly to the front door. Inside, it was clean enough, but the furnishings spoke of yard sales and cast-offs. Brent felt remorse, but it was his father who apologized to Ricky and his parents first.

"For my son to have done this, I've failed as a parent," Brent's father told the Lunsfords. "Anything I can do to set it right I will. The least we can do is pay two weeks' worth of Ricky's lunches."

His father had taken out his billfold and offered a twenty-dollar bill. Mr. Lunsford refused the money, but he and his wife accepted the apology. Mrs. Lunsford even made light of it, saying it was just boys being boys. Ricky and Brent shook hands. There had been no other punishment, but on the ride home Brent's father had said he wouldn't have believed Brent capable of such a thing, words left hanging in the dense silence. Brent still saw Ricky around town, but they kept their eyes down if they happened to pass each other.

Maybe if he had not been drunk, Brent wouldn't have set the fire. It had happened on the following Tuesday night, the day after his father had given up on any kind of litigation. They were building a deck for a retired dentist from Charlotte. They'd done jobs for the man before and he paid without wrangling over the price, as his father reminded Brent when he insisted they not take another job without a contract that a lawyer had double-checked.

"At least a contract for people we don't know," Brent argued, but his father hadn't replied and Brent knew there was nothing left to say.

That night he and Leslie watched a movie, but afterward, when Leslie went to bed, Brent didn't follow. He'd drunk three beers, his usual limit, but he got three more from the refrigerator and went outside to sit in the swing. In a few minutes the bedroom light went off, but the porch and living room lights still shone. Moths swirled around the porch's bare bulb, but the rackety air conditioner displaced the night's sounds. Six months back, Cam Beecham had offered to sell them this house and two-acre lot, but Beecham was asking a thousand more than the county appraisal. Brent and Leslie had believed he would lower his asking price, but there'd been no new offer.

Brent finished the fifth beer, crumpled the can, and tossed it to the ground. He tightened his hands around the bright steel chains, swayed back and forth a few moments. When he and Leslie had moved in, Brent had noticed that the grass wasn't worn beneath the swing seat, put up and left as if a taunt. His mind went to the dock and stayed there. When Brent was growing up, his father would point out how a plumber in Sylva had done shoddy work but then gone out of business, or how a county clerk embezzled money for three years but ended up in prison. It catches up with you, son, he'd say. But plenty did get away with it, Brent knew. All you had to do was look at the recession, which almost caused him and his father to lose everything.

The silk-tied crooks who'd done it weren't arrested and no one pretended they ever would be. People like that got away with anything. Get caught robbing folks, all you had to do was pay back part of what you stole. Turn a million people into drug addicts, you didn't spend a day in jail.

Brent threw the last can into the weeds and went to the shed for the gas can and a flashlight. The matches were in the Escort's glove compartment. He didn't switch on the headlights until he'd reached the end of the driveway and turned onto the blacktop. Leslie had the radio tuned to an easy-listening station, so Brent stabbed the buttons until something loud and relentless pulsed the speakers.

He pulled off the road at the end of Hewitt's drive and walked down to the lake. The moon and stars were out and he hardly needed the Maglite. All was dark inside the house. Brent soaked the planks and railing with gasoline and stepped back onshore. The first match went out but the second caught. Flames sprinted across the wood. Smoke rose and began obscuring the stars. When Brent got to the car, he saw a bright yellow tongue lapping the water.

The next morning he was in the shower when Sheriff Honeycutt knocked on the door and told Leslie he needed to talk to Brent. Just a matter that needs clearing up, Sheriff Honeycutt answered when Leslie asked why. He waited outside as Brent dressed.

"I called your dad and he's meeting us at the courthouse," the sheriff said when Brent came out on the porch. "Aubrey Hewitt's already there. That dock you built him was set on fire last night."

"And you think I did it?" Brent asked.

The sheriff raised his hand, palm out as he might halt a car.

"Hewitt thinks it, either you or your father," Honeycutt answered, lowering his hand. "I'd say there's plenty of folks wished they'd done it, including fishermen who bring their boats into that cove. Hewitt calls me and Willie Bost at Fish and Game complaining about them. Like Willie says, the man buys two acres of waterfront and thinks he owns the whole damn lake."

Hewitt and his father waited on separate sides of the courthouse foyer. The room was otherwise vacant, and as the four of them walked across the worn marble to Honeycutt's office, their footsteps echoed.

"All right, Mr. Hewitt," the sheriff said, once they were all seated. "Have your say."

"They burned my dock down last night."

"We done no such thing," Brent's father answered.

"Maybe you didn't, as far as being there," Hewitt said, "but your son did and you know he did it. As I told you over the phone, Sheriff, that boy made a threat. 'You're going to pay for doing this to us.' Those were his exact words."

"He didn't say it that way," Brent's father said. "He said . . ."

But Sheriff Honeycutt raised his hand.

"Let's just deal with who set the dock on fire," he said, and looked at Brent's father, then Brent. "Were either of you near Mr. Hewitt's dock last night, or in a boat on the lake?"

"We don't even own a boat and we weren't around his dock," Brent's father answered. "You've known me long enough to know my word's good, Sheriff. You'll not find a man in this county who'll tell you otherwise, same for Brent."

"I've never had cause to disbelieve anything you've told me, Dale," Honeycutt said, turning to Hewitt.

"Even if he's telling the truth, that doesn't mean his son is," Hewitt said. "He's the one that threatened me, and I haven't heard him deny anything."

The three men settled their eyes on Brent.

"What do you say, son?" Honeycutt asked.

"I didn't set that fire," he answered. "I didn't even leave my house last night."

"He's lying," Hewitt said.

"If you call me a liar again," Brent said, "I'll give you real cause to hire a damn lawyer."

"There's no cause for talk like that, from either of you," the sheriff said, standing up. "I'll go up to your place and look around, Mr. Hewitt, but unless there's some material evidence that can be tied to these men, there's no cause to charge them. You didn't see anything such as a gas can on the bank, did you?"

"No," Hewitt replied, "but isn't that your job?"

"I just told you I'll look around," Sheriff Honeycutt answered tersely. "We know these men's footprints will be down there, but if someone else's are that might help me find who did this. But my guess is whoever it was came up by boat, probably one of those fishermen you keep harassing. You need to accept that as long as they stay in their boats they can come as close to your property as they like."

"Talk to them then," Hewitt said. "I gave you and the wildlife officer their boat numbers. Somebody had to have seen something. The way that dock was burning, it looked like the whole lake was on fire."

"I'll check with Fish and Game about any boats that might have been in the cove last night. If not, this isn't likely to get solved." Sheriff Honeycutt paused. "You know, Mr. Hewitt, you'd be doing yourself a favor by being less confrontational with people."

"So," Hewitt bristled. "It's my fault the dock was burned."

"I'm just saying it might prevent something like this from happening again."

"That's good advice the sheriff's giving you, Mr. Hewitt," Brent said, meeting the man's eyes. "Next time they might set a match to your house."

"There's no need for that kind of talk, son," Brent's father said, but the apprehension now clouding Hewitt's face made Brent think otherwise.

"You do this investigation right, Sheriff," Hewitt said as he stood. "I've got friends in Raleigh, people you're familiar with."

For the first time since he'd picked Brent up, Honeycutt smiled.

"Well then tell them hello for me, Mr. Hewitt."


"Sorry I had to bring you two in," the sheriff said after Hewitt left. "I never believed you all would do something like this, but I had to go through the motions."

"We understand," Brent's father answered.

"You can take Brent home, can't you?" Sheriff Honeycutt asked.

"Of course," his father said, and the two men shook hands.

As they walked out of the courthouse, Brent watched his father's tentative steps, remembered how pale and vulnerable his father's legs had looked last Friday.

They were halfway home before Brent's father spoke.

"That must have been a sight, a dock that long burning," he mused. "There's a lake of fire in the Book of Revelation. Preacher Orr was telling of it just a few weeks ago." Brent's father paused and gave a slight smile. "Of course, that lake is one you'd not want to be there to see, would you?"

"No, sir," Brent answered.

They turned off the main road and soon passed Mac's Bar and Grill. A single pickup was in the driveway, probably left by someone with the good sense to let a friend drive him home. Brent's heart quickened as he thought of how easily blue lights might have appeared in his own truck mirror last night.

"I expect you're feeling it's time for you to go out on your own," his father said.

The words were spoken in a matter-of-fact way, neutral in tone. Brent looked at his father's face, but it revealed nothing.

"How so?" Brent asked.

"Business."

"Not you and me," Brent answered, "just the way we do business."

"It's one in the same."

"It doesn't have to be, Dad," Brent said.

"No, for me it does. You're young. You and Leslie want to have a family. I want you to have that too, and a place of your own without fretting each month about whether you can pay the mortgage."

"We can work together," Brent answered. "We just have to change things to make sure we don't get screwed by assholes like Hewitt."

"No, I'll be working only a couple of more years," his father replied, "so I'll stick to my old ways."

"You sure?" Brent asked.

"You're better suited for how things are now," his father answered. "I've known that for a long while."

He glanced over at his father, but the older man looked straight ahead. There was nothing else to say. Soon Brent was thinking of the standard contract he'd have a lawyer ensure was airtight. Other things would be changed too. He'd cut some corners the way most builders did, jack the price up on material estimates. If he did these things, maybe it wouldn't be too long before he and Leslie did have a child and their own home. His father made the last turn. The swing set came into sight. Almost new, not a speck of rust, as if waiting for a child.

# Sad Man
# in the Sky

‡

As soon as I see him coming up the road, I'm thinking this fellow could be trouble. I figure he's hitchhiking, but his thumb stays down as the cars pass. He's wearing a saggy black tank top, blue jeans, and scuffed-up penny loafers. A pillowcase full of God knows what is slung over his shoulder. Homeless, ex-con, druggie, maybe all three. Keep on going, I'm thinking, but the man leaves the road, walks to where I sit on my truck's tailgate. There's a tattoo of a padlock on the center of his upper chest. It's right-sized but faded and off-plumb, a prison tat if ever I've seen one.

He's looking at the helicopter behind me in the pasture, maybe figuring any fellow who owns one would have cash enough to lay a ten or twenty on him. But if he's thinking of getting money from me he's dead wrong. I work ten-hour shifts Monday to Thursday. Then I'm here Friday afternoons flying Todd Watson's chopper to keep the bills paid and help out our two girls. If this guy decides to get feisty, there's a pipe wrench in the cab to handle that. But when he turns his eyes toward me, he doesn't look mean or drugged or drunk, just worn down. His whole body sags like even his bones have given up.

"How much?" he asks.

"How much for what?"

"To take me up in that thing."

It ain't a quarter so it's likely outside your price range is what I'm thinking, but instead I answer seventy-five each with two or more passengers and a hundred and twenty solo. I expect that to turn his feet back the way he came, but he doesn't even blink.

"And you'll take me where I want to go?" he asks.

"It's supposed to be what it says," I tell him, pointing at the SMOKEY MOUNTAIN PARK TOUR sign, "but I'll take you whatever direction you want as long as we're back here in thirty minutes."

He opens his billfold. The plastic photo sleeves are empty. He takes the bills out one at a time, first four twenties, then three tens and two fives. He's got a few bills left but most look to have George Washington on them.

"Maybe you ought to save that money for something else," I tell him, though not in a smart-alecky way.

"I reckon not," he answers, fetching a watch from his pocket.

He doesn't strike me as someone who needs to worry much about what time it is, but he gives the watch a careful look before putting it back. I notice it's 3:05, which tells me I've been out here three hours and had just four customers. Some leaf peepers are coming at five-thirty, but that may be it for the day. I take his money, eyeballing it good before putting it in my billfold.

"I can lock up your ruck if you want me to," I tell him.

"I figure to take it with me," he answers. "It don't weigh but a few pounds."

"It's not the weight," I answer. "I need to know what's inside. I don't let folks bring just anything onboard."

"Presents," he says, and opens the pillowcase to show four packages wrapped in bright-red paper.

"It's a bit early in the year to play Santa Claus, ain't it?"

He pulls out his watch again.

"We need to go," he says.

So we get in and buckle up. I hand him his mic and headphones, disengage the rotor brake, and mash the starter. When the blades get spinning good, I press the pedal and the skids lift free of the earth. As always, memories of long-ago flights tense my stomach. Then I settle myself and am fine. I look over at my passenger and ask where he wants to go.

"Sawyer Ridge," he says, pointing across the river.

It's like warning signals just lit up on the instrument panel, because Sawyer Ridge is a place most people don't want anything to do with. Some good folks live there, but so do enough mean ones to fill up the county newspaper's arrest report. They're the sort who don't much like anyone snooping around where they live. To them, the bird would make a dandy target for some rifle practice. I had enough of getting shot at in the army so I tell him there's more interesting places to see, but he shakes his head.

A deal's a deal so I point the nose that way. Soon we are above the town, where the traffic's picked up since school's letting out. We fly over the Baptist church's steeple and then over the courthouse. As we cross the river I see some folks fishing. It's October, so there's red and yellow leaves lining the big pools where the water slows.

Soon Sawyer Ridge comes into view and the man points at the highest peak. We pass above some trailers and a few small farmhouses. Most folks look to be at work or inside, but we fly over a woman out in her garden, a couple of fellows bent over a car engine. We're near the ridge top when he points at a small house on the left side of the road.

"I want you to fly right over that house," he says.

I do what he asks even as I scan the trees for the glint of a rifle barrel. As we get closer, I see where the paint's peeled off the sides of the house. The front yard is just dirt with a few scabs of grass, in the side yard a swing set and a clothesline. There's toys scattered around the yard, but no trash and junk. I drift a bit and see a ladder leaning against the back of the house, a fresh coat of white paint on the upper half. Whoever lives here looks to be living hard, but they haven't given up.

"They ain't home yet," the man says.

You could have found that out a lot cheaper with a phone call, I'm thinking. He says for me to stay where we are, just nods when I say it still counts on his thirty minutes. So we hover above the house like a big dragonfly. A good five minutes pass before I see a yellow school bus coming up the road. It stops in front of the house and a boy and girl get out, their backpacks near big as they are. The bus chugs on up the road. Only then do the kids hear the copter and look up. They start waving, the way children always do. I look over at the man. He's got the pillowcase in his lap and he's sliding down the window.

"What are you doing?" I yell into the mic.

"Throwing these out," he answers.

"You ain't throwing anything out that window," I say, and ease the cyclic forward to make the hover turn. The kids and house are quickly out of sight. I'm headed back toward town. All sorts of thoughts are storming up in my head and none of them good.

"It's just presents for the kids," he says as the river appears below us. "Just some things I wanted to give them."

"Presents?" I say. "How do I know they're not drugs in those packages?"

"I'd never hurt them kids," he says. "I can show you they're just presents. Please, mister, just let me show you."

"Even if it is just presents, there's laws against people dropping things out of helicopters."

"You need to understand," the man says. "I've got to do this. Those children, they're . . ."

He stops and I see his eyes getting teary.

"We're gonna have to talk about this," I tell him.

I head upstream where there's a campground with an asphalt parking lot. I don't see a green ranger Jeep and the lot's not crowded, so I lower the collective and set her down.

"Show me one of those presents," I say when the big blades still.

"It's a ball and glove for my boy," he says, and hands me the package.

It's a piss-poor wrapping job, a bunch of tape and wrinkled paper. I feel the leather beneath the paper, the baseball's roundness in the glove's pocket. I make sure there's nothing else and hand it back to him.

"Let's see the others."

"It's one of them Cabbage Patch dolls from down in Georgia," he says, holding the next present out to me.

This one's wrapped thicker, but I can feel the plastic head and soft body. I check every inch of it to make sure nothing's sewn inside. The next two gifts are in boxes. He peels back the tape and paper.

"The woman at the store claims young girls were big on these," he says, opening a white box. Inside is a silver charm bracelet. He opens the last package and holds up a plastic figurine. "It's called a Power Ranger."

He retapes the presents as best he can and puts them in the pillowcase.

"So you going to take me?"

"You mind me asking you why you don't take those presents up there yourself?"

"I can't be around them no more," he says.

I look at him hard.

"Did you hurt those kids?"

"I'd not deny I hurt them and their momma too, but not the way you're thinking."

"How then?" I ask.

"I did something after I promised not to."

"What was that?"

"Got weak and gave in to the craving."

"Drugs, you mean."

"Yes."

"But if they're your kids and you've served your time . . ."

"They ain't mine by blood," he says. "Their real daddy took off and left them. They was three and five when I moved in. I ain't done much good in my life, but I tried hard to be a good daddy. For a while I was."

"She got a restraining order against you?"

"No."

He turns and looks out the window and I figure he's had his say but not yet.

"After I got out I went over to Tennessee. My uncle's got a body shop there and gave me work. I've been clean for a year so figured she might give me another chance. I called but hardly got a word out before she told me she's with another man now, that he don't do drugs or drink and holds down a steady job. She said he treats the kids great and if I really loved them as much as I claimed I'd never come near them again. She told me I'd had my chance."

"You don't think those kids will know who they're from?"

"I didn't put in a card or note, and they won't see me clear enough in this helicopter. Their mom might know, but she won't tell them."

I already know what I'm going to do, but it has nothing to do with him.

"Okay," I say.

As we head back to Sawyer Ridge, I try not to think about how many NAB regulations I'm about to violate. The kids aren't outside when I settle over the house. He drops the ball and glove first. It lands in the front yard, hitting so hard the paper splits open. The doll hits the roof and slides off into the yard. The last gifts land as the boy and girl run out of the house. We watch as they gather up the presents. Then I pivot and head back.

We cross the river and pass over the high-stilted water tower and the school. Soon we're back on the ground. I cut the engine. We sit a while longer, lost in our own thoughts.

"Listen," I finally say, taking two twenties and a five

from my billfold. "I don't feel right charging you more just because you went solo."

"I knew the price ahead of time."

"It'd make me feel better if you took it."

He puts the cash in his billfold and we get out. No one's waiting to take a ride so I ask if he needs me to drive him somewhere.

"I'm just down the road at the Super Eight," he says. "It'll be good to stretch my legs a bit before the bus ride back to Tennessee."

"When do you leave?"

"Tonight."

We stand there a while longer. I try to think of something to say, but nothing comes. All the while I'm staring at his tattoo, though I don't realize it until he lifts a hand and touches it.

"I hoped it might keep things out," he says, "but all it seems to do is keep them in."

He stuffs the pillowcase in his back pocket, walks out to the road, and heads back toward town. In a few minutes my first group of leaf peepers come and a while later the second. By the time we land, Todd Watson and his oldest boy are waiting. I don't mention the man and the presents, just hand Todd the checks and bills, tell him I've already taken forty-five out of my share. We settle up for the rest. Then I get in my truck and head home.

Fay's getting dinner ready, so I put the money on my bureau and join her in the kitchen.

"Did the girls call?" I ask.

"Bobby Jo did."

"Any news?"

"Hal's got a new line shift supervisor," Fay says. "Jessica's trying out for the basketball team. That's about it."

"You didn't hear from Dena?"

"Got an email," Fay says. "She told me she's doing fine, just having to work extra hours on a project."

It's Friday night but Fay has to work in the morning, so she goes on to bed. I drink a beer and watch a little TV. I'm tired but I know sleep won't come easy tonight. At eleven I lock the doors and go to bed. I snuggle up close and put my arms around her.

"That alarm goes off early for me," she says.

"It ain't about that," I answer.

Fay's body settles deeper into mine and she's soon back asleep, but I'll be awake awhile. Too many memories have gotten stirred up, including times I was in the air wondering if I'd ever see my family again. But that's not what's most on my mind. I'm thinking about those two kids and how, unlike all the other children I watched from above, they were running toward, not away from, what might rain down from the sky.

# L'homme Blessé

‡

Every month there were two or three phone queries like this one. Someone had bought a Monet at a yard sale in Weaverville or found a Grecian urn in a woodshed. One unhinged caller claimed he'd discovered the missing arms of the *Venus de Milo*. Others wanted Jake to evaluate folk art, hoping some elderly relative might be the new Grandma Moses or Howard Finster. A few showed up at the college unannounced, treasure trove in hand, sent by a receptionist or administrator to him, Brevard's only art teacher. Most could be persuaded to seek evaluations by museums or galleries, though sometimes, out of personal curiosity or their insistence, Jake agreed to examine what they had. If nothing else, the consultations fulfilled his department's community-outreach requirement, which would help next year when he came up for tenure.

This time the art was too large to bring to campus, which meant a twelve-mile drive to an isolated farmhouse, but it was an excuse to miss his afternoon office hours, which so late in the semester meant students either arguing or begging for higher grades. He was too tired to face them. Besides, the caller was Shelby Tate, whom he'd taught last fall. A good student—smart, serious, a bit older than most. She'd mentioned the paintings in class one day. Her great-uncle had covered every wall in his bedroom with painted portraits of strange beasts, her comment garnering odd looks from the other students. Jake was curious and planned to go see them during the Christmas break, but what had happened to Melissa changed all that.

Jake locked his office and walked to the faculty lot. Across the way, a grounds crew hung a wreath above the dining room door, a reminder to stop by CVS when he returned. He headed west on Highway 19, the directions on the passenger seat. The leaves were off the trees now, revealing time-worn swells so unlike the wild, seismic peaks and valleys beloved by European Romantics such as Pernhart and Friedrich. Sturm und Drang. Yet the Appalachians were daunting in their uniformity, a vast wall, unmarked by crevices that might provide an easy path out.

When the odometer neared twelve miles, Jake watched for the red realty sign marking where to turn. Gravel first, then dirt leading to a bridgeless stream. He pressed the brake, might have turned and gone back home if not for the urgency in Shelby's voice. *Please, Dr. Yancey. If you don't come now, it'll be too late.* As the car splashed across, a back wheel spun for a moment before gaining traction. The woods opened up and a small house came into view, most of its paint peeled off, the tin roof pocked with rust. A red Jeep Wrangler was parked in front of the porch. Shelby came out to greet him. Although she wore sweatpants and an oversized sweatshirt, her pregnancy was evident. Her eyes were the same light blue as Melissa's had been, which he'd either forgotten or not noticed before.

"Thank you for coming, Dr. Yancey," Shelby said, her accent more noticeable than he remembered. "I'm sorry to call you so sudden, but Daddy sold this place yesterday. The new owner's going to raze this house next week."

"It wasn't a problem," he answered. "It gives me a break from listening to students complain about grades, something you never needed to do. You made an A, I recall."

"Yes sir, I did," Shelby answered, and hesitated. "I wasn't certain you were still at the college, but I'm glad you are."

For a few moments, neither of them spoke.

"Well," Shelby said, nodding toward the open door. "What I wanted you to see is inside. Watch that first porch step. It's so rotten it might give way on you."

A lantern was beside the door, and Shelby struck a match and lit the wick.

"There's no electricity," she said.

He followed her into the front room. As his eyes adjusted to the muted light, Jake saw dusty pieces of furniture, a fireplace holding a few charred logs. They walked through a small kitchen and then down the narrow hallway. Shelby paused at a bedroom door on the left.

"In here, Dr. Yancey," she said, raising the lantern as they entered.

*Strange beasts, indeed,* Jake thought, his gaze drifting across the walls. The images were amateurish but discernible. A zebra with red spots instead of stripes, a small spiked fin on its back, a shaggy elephant with down-curving tusks, a deer with the snout of an anteater, a thin-legged boar. Plywood had been nailed over the single window frame, on it in calligraphic black the face of a lion. Except for a moldering mattress on the floor, the room was bare. But as Jake's eyes adjusted, the animals became more distinct. A mastodon, not a hairy elephant; a bison, not a boar. Despite the fin, the spotted horse too was familiar.

"I've seen these images before," Jake mused aloud.

"Where?" Shelby asked.

"A book on ancient art. They were inside a French cave."

"A French cave?" Shelby asked, clearly puzzled. "That seems so unlikely."

"Why?"

"How would Uncle Walt know about paintings like that?"

"Same as me, I imagine, from an art history book."

"But he didn't have any art books."

"Then television, or a magazine."

"Uncle Walt didn't have a television, and once he got back from World War Two Daddy says he hardly left this place. Twice a month Grandfather drove him to town to shop and cash his Social Security and VA checks, but that was it."

"When did he paint these?" Jake asked.

"Daddy says it was right after he came back from Europe."

The images did appear that old, the red and black paint flecked, the lion fading into the warped and rotting plywood.

"Maybe he saw the images over there."

Shelby shrugged.

"Maybe."

"When did he die?"

"2001."

"Did he paint any besides these?"

"Not that I know of."

"So during the war, he was in France?"

"I know he was at D-Day," Shelby said, and nodded at the animals. "I used to think it was what he saw in his nightmares, but if it was, why did he sleep in here all those years?"

"Maybe he needed to confront it," Jake said. "Was there ever a bed in here?"

"No, just the mattress. Daddy thinks that had something to do with the war, needing to be closer to the floor, feel less exposed. When I was a kid and we came to visit, Uncle Walt let me jump on it, like it was a trampoline. He was always kind to us kids. A couple of times I got spooked being alone back here, so I'd go out front with the grown-ups."

"A folk art dealer or museum might find these walls interesting," Jake said, "but with the paintings so faded, and trying to get them out without the plaster crumbling, I doubt . . ."

"I know, but it's not why I asked you to come. Daddy's having to sell this place because the taxes are a burden. Before they tear the house down, I wanted at least one person besides Uncle Walt's kin to see the paintings, someone who might appreciate his doing them."

In the last week, the exhaustion and lack of sleep had made his emotions so raw. Now, despite the Klonopin, he blinked back tears. Jake took out his phone, busied himself with it. Only one bar appeared.

"I was going to pull up some of the cave images."

"There's no reception out here," Shelby said, and smiled,

"which isn't always a bad thing. I get a few whiners about grades too, not the students but their parents."

"Which grade?"

"Fifth," she answered. "Most of the kids are real sweet and I'll miss them when I'm on maternity leave."

"Mind if I take a couple of pictures?" Jake asked.

"No."

Jake took one of each wall before putting the phone back in his pocket.

"I'll compare them when I get back to the office. Like I said, maybe he saw photographs in France, if not in a book then a magazine or newspaper."

"You don't have to do that," Shelby said. "The main thing was just you seeing them."

They looked at the walls a few more moments. The images were not originals like the wild bestiaries of a folk artist like Robert Burnside, nor was there some stylistic quirk. More like something copied from a book by a talented child, but as Jake stared at them he was moved that the man felt such a deep need to express what he'd endured. They walked up the hallway and onto the porch. Shelby closed the door but did not lock it.

"If you give me your number I'll text or call if I find out something," Jake said, pausing as Shelby wrote her number on a scrap of paper. "Thank you for the card you sent after Melissa died. I should have responded, but, anyway, this visit allows me to say it now."

"I've thought about calling you for months," Shelby said, "but figured you had a hard enough time without burdening you more. But with the sale . . ."

"I'm glad you called," he said.

As Jake drove back to Brevard, the name of the cave lingered just on the edge of memory. Not one word like Lascaux or Chauvet, but two words. Just outside the Brevard city limits, a Subaru wagon came up fast behind him, tied to its roof a Christmas tree, its tip pointed at him like a spear. A black tide of memory washed over him.

December 14, almost exactly a year ago, he and Melissa had been decorating for a Christmas party, three other couples invited. Melissa had gotten a promotion and Jake's division chair had mentioned that his chances for tenure were excellent, so there was much to celebrate. They had gone all out: holly on the fireboard, a Fraser fir wreath. Melissa had been setting the table when the forks slipped from her grasp and clattered against the floor. She placed a hand on the table to steady herself and told Jake she was dizzy. A day later Melissa was dead. In the hospital room, he had lifted a hand heavy and cold as clay.

Shelby was one of two students who sent a card, one likely picked up at a CVS or grocery store, the card's condolences followed by a handwritten sentence about his being in her thoughts and prayers. A brevity Jake appreciated. He'd been amazed at what people, intelligent people, could utter at such a time. An English professor, his wife beside him, quoted Tennyson's "better to have loved and lost, than never to have loved at all." Another colleague said, "It's good you two decided not to have children," and yet another told Jake that at least he was young enough "to find another wife and start over," as if Melissa were simply a defective machine part easily replaced.

———

When he got back to his office, no one else was around. Jake left the lights off, the only glow that of the computer screen as he tapped in "cave art France." After a few clicks the bison, mammoth, and lion appeared. The spotted zebra was there too, though it was actually a horse. What Jake had thought a fin was instead a human hand hovering over the animal. Pech Merle was the cave's name. He pulled up an article about its discovery in 1922. Black-and-white photographs showed the first scientists exploring the cave.

When they were in grad school together, Mason Bromwich's dissertation had been on cave art, so Jake typed a message noting how the paintings were identical to those in Pech Merle, adding that the man who'd done them was in France during World War II.

MY QUESTION IS THIS, Jake typed. THE CAVE'S IMAGES WOULD BE IN FRENCH MAGAZINES AND NEWSPAPERS AT THAT TIME, CORRECT?

Jake hesitated. The email's timing might be perceived as a subtle outreach for sympathy, for an invitation. Or seen for what it was, a request for information.

A STUDENT WANTS TO KNOW, he typed, and hit send.

He didn't expect an immediate reply and was about to shut off the computer and leave when Mason's response came.

HI, BUDDY, LONG TIME, NO HEAR. YOU NEED TO ANSWER YOUR EMAILS!! RE PAINTINGS—BY DETAILS, YOU MEAN EVEN THE COLORS ARE RIGHT?

YES, Jake typed. ORANGE BISON, RED DOTS ON THE HORSES.

LET ME CHECK A FEW THINGS IN SOME BOOKS. NEED IT SOON?

Jake's hand paused over the keyboard.

YES, he typed.

GIVE ME A FEW MINUTES AND I'LL GET BACK TO YOU. YOU DOING OK? I KNOW IT'S PROBABLY NOT AN EASY TIME OF YEAR FOR YOU.

I'M FINE.

Jake leaned back in his chair and waited. Footsteps came down the hallway, a familiar clack of heels. Jake was glad his office light was off. If not, Lila Marshall would stop and want to chat. She'd recently gone through a divorce and felt she and Jake were kindred spirits. There are worse ways to lose your spouse than through death, she'd once told him. Lila's office door opened but soon closed again. Her heels echoed hollowly back down the hall and she was gone. Half an hour passed before Mason's response came.

YOUR SOLDIER DIDN'T SEE THEM IN A MAGAZINE OR NEWS-PAPER. I EMAILED MARC VALERY AND HE AGREED THAT THE BEST SOURCES SAY NO COLOR PECH MERLE PHOTOGRAPHS BEFORE 1951, EVEN IN ART BOOKS, MUCH LESS NEWSPAPERS OR MAGAZINES. (THAT'S IN FRANCE OR ANYWHERE ELSE.) THE ONLY WAY TO KNOW ALL THOSE DETAILS WOULD HAVE BEEN VISITING THE CAVE ITSELF. M

Jake typed a response.

I DOUBT HE'D BE WANDERING AROUND IN CAVES. THEY WERE FIGHTING A WAR.

THEN SOMEONE'S FIBBING ABOUT WHEN THE IMAGES WERE PAINTED.

I DON'T THINK SO. THE PAINTINGS APPEAR THAT OLD.

MAYBE COLOR PHOTOGRAPHS WERE TAKEN, BUT A GI COMING UPON THEM? IT'S A STRETCH, PAL. CHECK TROOP MOVEMENTS. IF ANYTHING, THEY MIGHT HAVE PASSED THROUGH THE AREA.

THANKS FOR THE HELP.

NO PROBLEM, JAKE. SERIOUSLY, YOU DOING OKAY?

I'M OKAY.

JANICE AND I WOULD LOVE TO HAVE YOU COME UP FOR CHRISTMAS.

THANKS, BUT I'LL JUST STICK AROUND HERE.

JANICE PROMISED TO BUY YOU A STOCKING AND HANG IT UP WITH KELLY'S, AND YOU KNOW MY CHEF CREDENTIALS. WHAT YOU SAY?

MAYBE ANOTHER TIME.

OKAY, BUT IF YOU CHANGE YOUR MIND . . .

OKAY. GOT TO GO. THANKS AGAIN.

Jake sat awhile longer, summoning the energy to get up, to walk to the lot, to turn the key in the ignition. The gas could wait but not the prescription, so he drove to the CVS. Inside, Christmas reds and greens dominated, but holiday cheer was absent. It was near closing and the employees looked tired and harried. The store's harsh fluorescent lights seemed designed to heighten such unhappiness. *If you don't stay, you won't get even a few hours' sleep tonight*, he reminded himself.

The customer at the counter turned and dropped her prescription into a bag decorated with candy canes, shifting time: a red stocking filled with shiny foiled Hershey's kisses, bright-striped candy canes, tangerines, and, at the bottom, a box of crayons. Jake must have been four, because he wasn't yet in kindergarten. He remembered the crayons' waxy smell as the colors and shapes flowed unmediated from his hand to paper. The wonder of the act remained.

Before leaving, he made a couple more purchases. Once home, he tapped in Shelby's number.

"I asked Daddy again and he's certain the paintings were done in 1945," she said. "He said the paint cans are still in his shed and prove it."

"I'm not doubting your father," Jake said. "My friend says the only explanation is that your great-uncle was in the actual cave. Did he ever hear anything like that?"

"I never heard of it, but I can ask Daddy and call you back."

"Sure, I'll be up till at least eleven."

Jake listened to a message his sister had left about holiday plans, then poured a glass of wine. He'd finished a second glass when the cell rang. He checked the number and picked up.

"Daddy said Uncle Walt never talked about the war or France to him, and hardly to my grandfather either. But there's a man in Tennessee who was in the same unit. He visited Uncle Walt a few times, came to the funeral too. Daddy had his address and made some calls. He's at the VA hospital in Knoxville. I'm thinking about visiting him Saturday. It might be the only chance to talk to someone who knew Uncle Walt during the war. Having a child, it makes things like that seem more important." Shelby paused. "You'd be welcome to come along."

Jake had no plans for Saturday morning, other than a faculty luncheon he'd just as soon miss.

"I'd like that. What time and where?"

"Knoxville's three hours away, so is ten all right?" she asked. "We could meet at Uncle Walt's or in Brevard."

"I'll meet you at your Uncle Walt's," Jake said. "I'd like to see those paintings one more time. And can you give your father a quick call and see if he knows which division your uncle was in?"

"He'd know because he's got the discharge papers, but Daddy's likely asleep now. I'll find out tomorrow."

As Jake finished the wine he scanned the Internet for more images of the cave, finding some that were not on the farmhouse wall, including one of a man leaning or falling. Vertical lines—spears, perhaps arrows—passed through the figure's torso. Jake read the article, which suggested interpretations based on shamanism, the image's coloration, and its location within the cave. He shut down the computer and took the Ambien.

Jake awoke at three, feeling the same chest tightness that had sent him to the school infirmary last week. After an electrocardiogram showed nothing, Jake was given a scrip for Klonopin. *Don't hesitate to use it, Jake,* Dr. Wells had told him. He knew he wouldn't go back to sleep, so he made some coffee, then waited at the kitchen table for dawn to lighten the window above the sink. He showered and dressed, afterward drove to the college to teach his last classes of the semester.

On Saturday morning he arrived at the farmhouse on time, but it was ten-twenty before Shelby showed up.

"Sorry," she said. "I stopped to pick up some baby clothes from my sister."

"No problem," Jake said. "I can drive if you like."

"No, I don't mind. Plus, I know a shortcut to 40 even the GPS can't figure out."

As Jake opened the passenger door, Shelby nodded at a white pastry box, asked if he wanted her to put it in the back. Jake told her it was fine.

Soon they were on back roads Jake had never traveled.

"Have you met this man?" he asked.

"Once when he visited, but he probably won't remember me. His name is Ben Winkler."

They rode in silence awhile. A green sign appeared with the words I-40 West Knoxville/Chattanooga, and they merged onto the interstate.

"Have you decided on names for your child yet?" Jake asked.

"It's a boy and we're calling him Brody. It's a family surname."

"I like your using a last name that way," Jake said. "My wife and I were planning to have children, and wanted to do the same."

After they signed in at the front desk, the receptionist pointed to the elevator.

"Fifth floor. Take a right. It's room 507."

The door was open. Mr. Winkler sat in a recliner in the corner, a folded newspaper on his lap. A metal walker stood in front of the chair, green tennis balls on the wheels. After they introduced themselves, Winkler removed a pair of black glasses and set them and the paper on a lamp table. He rubbed the paunchy flesh below his eyes a moment, then motioned toward two plastic chairs. Shelby set the white box on the room's single bureau before sitting down.

"Pull those chairs closer," he said. "My hearing ain't what it used to be."

Jake and Shelby moved nearer.

"So you're Walt's niece?"

"Yes, sir," Shelby said. "Great-niece, that is."

For a few minutes Shelby made small talk with Mr. Winkler, asking about his health, the family pictures on the bureau. Her manner was unhurried and respectful. Though only thirty-six, Jake felt a huge gulf existed between him and his most recent students. He wondered if Shelby's generation was the last raised to tolerate quietness and stillness. It wasn't a judgment, just a reality. Perhaps a life of unyielding distraction was better, he'd often thought since Melissa's death.

"We have a question for you," Shelby said, "about Uncle Walt during the war."

"I'll try to answer," the old man responded. "But my memory's gotten near bad as my hearing and eyesight."

"When you were in France," Jake asked, "do you remember anything about a town called Cabrerets?"

"Hard to know," the older man said. "Most times we was too busy trying not to get shot to be looking for town signs."

"Yes, sir, I can imagine so," Jake said, taking out the map he'd printed off the Internet. "I looked up the troop movements, and it seems your division wasn't anywhere near there, but I wanted to be sure. The red mark I made, that's where the town was."

Mr. Winkler put his glasses back on, took the map and studied it.

"Some of us did come through there, not during the war but right after."

"Right after?"

"Yes. We had a three-day leave and took a train out of Paris. Walt hadn't wanted to go. He was in a bad way. We finally convinced him it might do him some good. The train was headed toward Toulouse, if I remember right, but we got off when the notion took us. Anyways, at one stop this Frenchman come on board jabbering about something we might want to see, said he'd drive us there and back."

"It was a cave, wasn't it?" Jake asked.

Winkler took off the glasses again and set them on the table. He looked at Shelby.

"Walt told about being in that cave?"

"No, sir, not that I know of," Shelby answered. "Were you in there with him?"

"Not the first time. I wanted to flirt with them French girls instead of visiting some old cave, but Walt and a couple of fellows went to see it. The others caught back up with us and said it wasn't worth the time, that they'd seen better drawings in the funny papers. When we asked where Walt was, they didn't know."

A smile creased the old man's face, his eyes no longer focused on his visitors but something more inward.

"We figured he'd got one of them French girls to say *oui*," Mr. Winkler said. "Anyways, when it was near time to catch the next train, we started searching. It come to nothing until a Frenchman said Walt was in the way-back part of that cave, laying on the ground, asleep. So me and another fellow went in to get him. It was spooky in there, I tell you that, and got spookier the deeper we went, and we went a long, long ways. It had to be near a mile. Darker than any place I ever been, and what light we had showing these old-time fierce animals on the walls. When we finally found Walt, he was laying on the cave floor asleep." Winkler stopped and looked at Shelby. "Your uncle was a brave man. I don't want you to feel otherwise about him."

"I won't," Shelby answered. "You can tell us."

"We woke him but he wouldn't get up. One of the fellows sat down beside Walt and tried to talk sense to him. But that done no good. He started crying and saying that the only thing outside of that cave was death. We finally had to grab his arms and drag him. Even then he kept begging us to leave him there."

"So he was at the very back of the cave?" Jake asked.

"Deep into that cave as you could get. I didn't think we'd ever get him out. The next week Walt was headed home on a Section Eight. Some fellows in the unit thought bad of him for breaking down like that, but none of them was in that first wave at Omaha Beach. Walt was in the 116th Infantry. You know about them?"

"No, sir," Jake answered.

"Well, they was in the thickest of it. Walt and two others from his unit came off that beach alive. Our outfit had some hard tussles, and Walt fought good as any man, but even then you could tell he was in a bad way. And every day it got worse."

"My daddy said Uncle Walt was never the same when he returned," Shelby said softly.

"None of us were, child," Winkler said, shaking his head. "It's just some could handle it better than others, or at least pretend to. My boys wanted me to go back over there a couple of years ago. They'd pay the flight, hotel, meals, everything. I told them thanks but that I'd spent most of my life trying to forget ever being there once."

The nurse who'd been waiting beside the door came into the room.

"It's time for your lunch, Mr. Winkler."

Shelby nodded at the white box on the bureau.

"I baked you some gingerbread cookies. You can have them for dessert."

"Thank you," he said, raising a trembling hand blotched purple-black. He held Shelby's hand a few moments before releasing it. "Your uncle, he was a good man. We didn't do much talking when I visited, but if you've been through tough times together, you don't have to."

When Jake and Shelby got back to the farmhouse, Jake asked if he could see the paintings a last time.

"Of course," Shelby said, and lit the lantern.

They went down the dark hallway. As their eyes adjusted, the menagerie slowly emerged. Shelby set the lantern down and stepped close to the lion. She placed her hands on the plywood, wiggled it until the two remaining nails pulled free. She carefully leaned the plywood against the wall.

"What will you do with it?" Jake asked.

"I don't know," Shelby answered. "It wouldn't seem right not to save something, especially after today. I might put it in the nursery."

Shelby leaned to pick up the lantern. When she stood again, the window's suffusing light surrounded her. *Woman with Lantern,* Jake thought. Perhaps somewhere such a painting existed. If not, he thought, it should. For a few minutes they were silent. Though it was midafternoon, the room was darkening. The animals began receding, as if summoned elsewhere.

"I guess I'd better be getting home," Shelby said, "else Matt will start worrying."

Jake carried the plywood out and Shelby placed it and the lantern in the back of the Jeep.

He opened the trunk of his car, then took out the sketch pads and boxes of crayons he'd bought at CVS.

"A gift for your son," he said. "Maybe he will be an artist like his great-great-uncle."

Shelby set the gifts beside the lantern and plywood.

"Thank you," she said, giving him an awkward hug, "not just for the gifts but for helping me find out about the paintings."

"I was glad to do it. When your baby's born, I'd like to know."

"It won't be much longer," she said, giving her stomach a soft pat. "The doctor says the third week in January."

"Cézanne was born around that date. The twentieth, I believe."

"Maybe I'll aim for that," she said, smiling.

"Would you mind if I stayed a few more minutes?" Jake asked.

"No, sir," Shelby said, looking at the surrounding woods. "In the fall when the leaves turn, this cove is such a pretty place. Even now, there's a beauty about it."

After Shelby left, Jake went back inside. He looked at the animals for a few minutes, then lay down on the mold-

ering mattress. The springs creaked and a thin layer of dust
rose and resettled. He did not realize that he had fallen
asleep until he opened his eyes in darkness. He felt his way
through the house and out the door. In the day's last light,
Jake drove slowly to the creek, stopped at the water's edge.
Oak trees lined the opposite bank. In their upper branches,
mistletoe clustered like bouquets offered to the emerging
stars. He paused there a few more moments, then went on.

# The Baptism

Reverend Yates had awaited his coming, first for hours, then days and weeks. Now it was late December and winter had set in. When he'd lowered the metal well bucket, it clanged as if hitting iron. A leashed pitchfork, cast like a harpoon, finally broke the ice. He was bringing the water back to the manse when Jason Gunter came out of the woods on horseback. Reverend Yates took the bucket inside and returned with a shotgun that, until this moment, had never been aimed at anything other than a fox or rabbit.

Gunter saw the weapon but did not turn the horse. Even in the saddle the younger man swaggered, the reins loosely held, body rocking side to side. Not yet thirty, but already responsible for one wife's death, nearly a second.

"That's a mighty unneighborly way to be greeted," Gunter said, smiling as he dismounted, "especially by a man of the cloth."

"I figured it would be one you understood," Reverend Yates replied.

Gunter opened his frock coat to show the absence of knife or pistol.

"I didn't come for a tussle, Preacher."

Gunter was dressed in much the same attire he'd arrived in four years ago—leather boots and wool breeches, white linen shirt and frogged gray coat. As then, his hair was slicked back and glistening with oil, his fingernails trimmed, undarkened by dirt. A dandy, people had assumed, which caused many to expect Gunter to fail miserably when he'd bought the farm adjoining Eliza Vaughn's property. But that hadn't been the case at all. He had brought his wife with him, a woman clearly once attractive but now hunch-shouldered. Her eyes were striking, the color of wisteria, though she seldom raised them when in town. A month after they had come, she'd hanged herself from a crossbeam in the barn, or so the county sheriff concluded.

Reverend Yates lowered the shotgun so it rested in the crook of his arm, but the barrel still pointed in Gunter's direction.

"If it's about where Susanna is . . ."

"It ain't about knowing where she is," Gunter answered. "That's over and done with."

"What is it then?"

"I got need to be baptized."

When Reverend Yates didn't respond, the younger man quit smiling. For a few moments they stared at each other.

"If you want someone to baptize you," Reverend Yates said, "there are plenty of other preachers who can do it."

"Who said *I* wanted it?"

Gunter turned, placed two fingers in his mouth, and gave a sharp whistle. Eliza Vaughn and her fourteen-year-old daughter, Pearl, came out of the woods and stood silently beside the horse's haunches. Reverend Yates stared at Eliza questioningly, but she would not meet his gaze. Beneath a coat once worn by her husband, the woman shivered, and perhaps not just from the cold. Reverend Yates had warned her not to let Susanna marry Gunter, but despite what had happened to Gunter's first wife, Eliza did not stop the marriage. Widowed, she'd had the hardship of raising two daughters alone. Gunter was a broad-shouldered man strong enough to keep the farm running. The first wife's death hadn't been Gunter's doing, Eliza claimed. *He ain't never drank a drop of liquor,* she'd said, as if all men needed alcohol to summon their perfidy. After the marriage, Gunter helped support Eliza and Pearl, keeping them in firewood, helping plant and harvest crops, digging a new well.

But there had been a price. First a pumpknot swelling Susanna's left brow, then two weeks later an arm so wrenched out of the socket that it hung useless at her side for weeks. Susanna did not claim she'd bumped her head entering a root cellar or twisted her arm restraining a rambunctious cow. She offered no explanation, nor did her mother or sister, even after several women in the congregation, out of curiosity or compassion, inquired. Her lot in life was to suffer, Susanna appeared to believe. But on that Sunday, watching her wince each time she moved the arm, Reverend Yates told her it was not her duty to suffer. Even then, Susanna had said nothing. She'd turned and walked back through town, past the manse and up the wooded path to where Gunter waited.

"Is this about your daughter, Eliza?" Reverend Yates asked sharply. "Because if it is, I swore I'd never tell where she went, and I'll honor that, even with her own mother."

"It ain't about that hussy that you helped run off from

me," Gunter said, looking at Eliza. "You tell him. You're the one says I got to do it."

"I want you to baptize Mr. Gunter," Eliza said.

"Why would you want that, Eliza?" Reverend Yates asked.

"To marry Pearl," the widow answered softly.

"She's of a mind it'll wash any devilment right out of me," Gunter said. "I don't think much is in me, but it seems some folks do. Anyway, if getting doused puts a mother's mind at ease I'll abide it."

"Pearl is a child," Reverend Yates said. He looked at the girl, wrapped in a quilt she cinched tight around her neck. Like her mother, she stared at the ground.

"There's many been married at her age, Preacher," Gunter said. "There's one in your own congregation."

Reverend Yates looked at Pearl. She was not shivering, but her cheeks glowed from the cold. He had baptized her and Susanna on the same July Sunday five years ago. A thin, delicate child, one often sick. He remembered how light she'd felt as he took her in his arms and lowered her into the river.

"You and your mother come into the house, child."

"Nah," Gunter said. "We need to be getting back. Some of us has to work more than just on Sundays."

"Eliza," Reverend Yates said.

She looked at him now, her pale face blank.

"This Sunday, Preacher," Gunter said. "Douse me in the morning and me and Pearl will get the justice of the peace to marry us right after. I done got that set up."

"Our baptisms are held in warmer weather."

"I know for a fact you baptized Henry Cope last winter," Gunter challenged.

"He was dying," Reverend Yates answered. "Even then it wasn't this cold."

"I know that water will be cold," Gunter said, grinning now, "but I figure Pearl will warm me up real good later."

"It isn't just the water that cleanses a man," Reverend Yates answered. "It's what is in his heart."

"I know that, Preacher."

"What if I won't do it?"

"We'll go to Boone," Gunter answered. "There's more than one preacher in this county. Of course, that's a mighty long walk for these two gals, especially with the chance of more snow coming." Gunter turned and nodded at Eliza and Pearl. "Go on now," he said.

Reverend Yates watched mother and child disappear back into the woods, stepping in their earlier footprints, as if in Gunter's presence they dare not even disturb the snow.

"We'll be seeing you Sunday, Preacher," Gunter said, raising finger and thumb to tip his hat. He nodded at the shotgun. "I'm a forgiving man, maybe you ought be the same, especially since I wouldn't be needing a wife if you'd not meddled in another man's business."

"I know my business, Gunter," Reverend Yates replied, but the words sounded feeble.

"Good," Gunter replied. "Do it come Sunday."

Gunter jerked the reins and the horse turned. He kicked a bootheel against its flank and went back up the path. Even when Gunter was out of sight, Reverend Yates heard the crunching of snow under the horse's hooves. He stared

at the woods, the bare gray branches reaching upward as if
in lamentation.


Susanna had come in the middle of night, pounding
frantically on the front door. Looking out the window, he'd
seen her silhouetted behind a lantern's glow. When Reverend Yates ushered her in, he saw she was barefoot and
dressed only in a shift. Susanna raised the lantern to show
the purple bruises where his fingers had grasped.

"All I done was be late fixing his bath," Susanna
pleaded. "He said next time it'd be a rope around my neck,
not a hand. He'd do it, Reverend. You know he would."

"What would you have me do?"

"Get me away from here, someplace he'll never find
me."

"What of your mother and sister?"

The fear in Susanna's eyes dimmed.

"They ain't able to stop him from killing me," she
answered, a sudden coldness in her voice.

Whether she had or had not understood the intent of his
question, Reverend Yates would never know. She'd asked for
his help, he told himself, so how could he not give it? Was
there a relative who could take her in, he asked, not close by
but one out-of-state? Susanna nodded. Don't tell me where,
Yates said, just which state. He'd put a quilt around her
and they walked down the street to Marvin Birch's house.
The three of them had gone to Marvin's dry goods to purchase Susanna shoes, clothes, and undergarments, enough
to wear and also fill a carpetbag. Marvin was known as a
skinflint, but he refused any money. Which was all to the

good, because it left twenty dollars to give her after Reverend Yates paid for the ticket to Johnson City. She could get to her final destination from there, he'd told her.

Afterward, he'd returned home and waited for Gunter to show up, the shotgun by the door, unloaded, though Gunter would not know that. But it was Eliza who'd come on that October morning. Reverend Yates told her he didn't know where Susanna was and would swear so on a Bible if need be. Without another word, Eliza walked back up the path to her farm. Except for some glares when they'd passed each other in the street, Gunter did nothing. Perhaps he believed, as Reverend Yates feared, Susanna would return on her own. He'd seen it before, women or children fleeing and then returning not out of corporal need but some darker necessity. At such times, he feared some malevolent counterpoint to grace operated in the world. But Susanna had not returned. Gunter obtained a divorce on grounds of abandonment.

A polite knock interrupted Reverend Yates's reverie. Opening the door, he found four congregation members on his porch, in the forefront Marvin Birch. He invited them in. Marvin seemed reluctant, but the others eagerly left the cold, though no one sat when offered a chair.

"We have heard about Gunter's latest outrage," Marvin said. "If I had known this was the purpose of his divorce, I would have ensured Judge Lingard did not grant it. What Gunter proposes, surely you will not allow?"

"If you mean the marriage itself, I have no part in it. He says he will go to the justice of the peace."

"But the baptism," Marvin said. "What of it?"

"If I don't, Gunter told me he'll go elsewhere," Reverend Yates answered.

"But if you do so," Marvin sputtered, "it would mean the community condones this abomination."

"It was Eliza, a member of our congregation, not Gunter, who asked this of me."

"That is of no importance, Reverend," the storekeeper bristled. "Let them go elsewhere."

"He will make them walk there, Marvin, and in this weather such a trek could give a girl with her delicate constitution the whooping cough or influenza. Would you want that on your conscience?"

"Doubtful, I say," Marvin answered. "And if so, might not death be better for the child than being wedded to that blackguard?"

"There is something else," Reverend Yates said, his voice more reflective. "What if the act itself, despite Gunter's lack of sincerity, were to truly cleanse the man?"

For a few moments the men stared at the hearth, as if the flames might yield an answer.

"You believe Gunter capable of such change?" Marvin asked.

"No," Reverend Yates answered, "but God is capable. It is the mystery of grace. I cannot be true to my responsibilities if I doubt the possibility."

"But our responsibility as town elders is different, Reverend. We cannot permit this."

"So you question God's wisdom in worldly matters?"

"God allows us the ability to discern evil, Reverend, and the strength to defy it."

"Yet not in this matter," Reverend Yates replied, with less certainty than he would have wished. "Be assured, I have not made my decision lightly, gentlemen. I appreciate and understand your concern, but the baptism must be allowed."

The next morning at the service, Gunter sat with Eliza and Pearl on the back pew. Reverend Yates had contemplated altering the sermon he'd written out Thursday night, but found himself too vexed to do so. As planned, he spoke of Moses, and how he'd led his people to the Promised Land though unable to enter that place himself. He read the sermon with as little attentiveness as his congregation offered in their listening, Gunter's presence casting a pall over the whole church.

Reverend Yates did not announce the baptism. Instead, he waited until the church emptied except for Gunter, Eliza, Pearl, and himself.

"This weather, surely . . ."

"We got quilts and dry clothes, even a sheet if you ain't got me a gown," Gunter said. "I'm going to have a fire on the bank, too. Got my wood and kindling and flint rock already waiting. So we'll go on out there, Preacher. Have you a fire going so you don't catch cold."

Reverend Yates went to the manse and changed into the trousers and white linen shirt he always wore for baptisms. He put on a wool scarf and his heaviest overcoat. The water might rise to his hips, but the pants would dry quickly by the fire, so he took no change of clothes, only a drying cloth. The baptism pool was a quarter-mile away.

Reverend Yates saddled his horse and followed Eliza's and Pearl's footprints in the snow, unsurprised when the hoof-prints of Gunter's mount, which preceded the woman and child, merged with those of other horses.

The trail curved and the river lay before him. A man-high fire blazed at the forest's edge, stoked with enough wood to burn for hours. Pearl and Eliza huddled beside it, Gunter close by. Reverend Yates dismounted and tethered his horse to a dogwood branch sleeved with ice. The elders stood on the riverbank. In the crook of Marvin Birch's right arm was a rifle.

As Yates approached, Marvin stepped aside so he could see the river.

"Tell me that ain't a sign from God, Reverend," the store owner said, facing the river as well.

The river's deep bend that served as the baptism pool was completely iced over, the snow-limned surface unmarked but for the tracks of a single raccoon. Had Reverend Yates not known otherwise, he'd have thought a meadow or pasture lay before him.

"When have you ever seen it covered like this?" Marvin asked, his thumb on the rifle's trigger guard. "Never a one of us has. It's a sign to us all and I'll abide no man to profane it."

Reverend Yates turned and looked at Gunter, who appeared in deep reflection as he too stared at the frozen river.

"Marvin's right," another elder said. "It's surely a sign from God."

The other elders nodded their assent. For a few moments the only sound was the crackle of the fire.

"There will be no baptism today," Reverend Yates finally said.

Only then did Gunter rouse himself. He shook his shoulders as if to cast off some burden.

"It's just ice," he said, and walked to the river's edge. He placed a foot on the surface, pressed his boot heel more firmly until his full weight was upon it.

"You thought you could mock God, Gunter," Marvin said, "but now God's mocking you, and he's doing it for all the world to see."

"Fetch me a stout tree limb, woman," Gunter said to Eliza.

As Eliza turned from the fire, Marvin Birch stepped close to Gunter. He gripped the rifle on the upper stock and held it out.

"God won't let you break that ice even with this, Gunter," the store owner announced, nodding at the butt end, "and it made of hickory."

"We'll see about that, damn you," the younger man replied, grabbing the rifle barrel with both hands and thrusting the butt downward.

The sharp report of shattered ice was instantly followed by a louder crack. The sounds crossed the river, echoed back. Gunter still gripped the iron barrel. He appeared to stare down at it intently as gray smoke encircled his head. He gave a violent shudder and fell forward, the webbed ice opening to accept the body. Gunter slowly sank. Soon the only sign of him was the water's pinkish tinge.

————

After Gunter's death, the community made certain that Eliza and Pearl were cared for. Then, at sixteen, Pearl married Lewis Hampton, whose father owned the valley's best bottomland, ensuring Eliza as well as her daughter would never again go wanting. Susanna remained in Tennessee but she and her family visited yearly, even after her mother died. On such Sundays, the sisters and their husbands and children filled a pew.

To look upon such a sight from his pulpit was surely a sign of God's grace, Reverend Yates told himself, but on late nights he sometimes contemplated his silence when Marvin Birch offered the cocked weapon. Had his refusal to warn Gunter been a furtherance of God's will or a shunning of his own duty? Would he have held Gunter underwater until he drowned, or lifted Gunter back into the mortal world? On such nights the parlor became nothing more than shadows and silence, the manse's stillness widening beyond the walls into the vastness of the whole valley.

# Flight

The trouble had begun during her fourth month at the park. Until then most of the visitors had been hikers, older couples who tapped the ground with ornate walking sticks as they followed the two-mile loop. They smiled when they saw her and went on their way. Nevertheless, the best days were when it snowed or rained and fewer people were around.

But April brought those who fished. As Stacy had done with the hikers, she studied their behavior. The ones who cast in the stream's catch-and-release section drove late-model Jeeps and SUVs, wore waders and vests and carried long rods and shiny reels. *Anglers* was her word for them. The gentle way they removed the barbless hook reminded her of a pet being freed from its leash. When asked for their licenses, they sometimes tilted their heads or rolled their eyes. *You've seen my bamboo rod and Orvis vest,* the gesture meant, *you think I can't afford a twenty-dollar license?*

*Fishermen* drove pickups and older cars with dents and rusty mufflers. Such vehicles were often left unlocked, windows rolled down. Fishermen cast from shore and used closed-face spinning reels, often Zebco 202s. They stayed near the bridge where the hatchery truck made its weekly dump. Some even followed the truck from the hatchery. The trout barely hit the water before they were yanked out. Nevertheless, Stacy preferred these people to the others. To kill and eat their catch was a purer act, none of the pretend-play of being a predator.

When she saw the battered blue truck in the lot, windows down, bed filled with trash bags and beer cans, she assumed its owner to be a fisherman. But it was the expired license plate that made Stacy check for her ticket pad before walking down the trail. This was the trade-off for those winter hours of solitude, she'd begun to realize, and it would only get worse come summer. With picnickers, tourists, campers crowding the park, there would be times she'd have to go to the ridgetop, be above it all.

Stacy stepped onto the bridge. A man she didn't recognize fished below. He'd heard her boots on the wood planks but did not look up. Instead, he cranked in his line, checked his corn-draped hook, and cast sidearm to the head of the pool. She left the bridge and came down the trail. Farther downstream, an elderly couple fished where the water slowed and formed a deep run. She'd checked their licenses and stringers last week.

"I need to see your license, sir," Stacy said.

"I don't need one," he answered, his eyes on the line.

Once on level ground, Stacy saw that the man was over six feet tall. He had a gut but thick-muscled arms, a stubbled chin that shadowed a centipede-shaped scar. The ball cap, jeans, and T-shirt were what many of the bait fishermen wore. Only the footwear surprised her. Instead of work boots, he had on black dress shoes.

"I need to check your fishing license," Stacy said again.

"I told you I don't need one," the man said, still not looking at her. "So you can be on your way."

She had already issued seven citations in the last two weeks—no license, too many fish. But no confrontations, only a couple of pleas of *Can't you let it go this time?* But she was issued a Glock for a reason. Stacy felt the gun's presence, that extra weight, on the side of her hip. Her instructors had emphasized that most rangers would never need to unholster their weapon. If it appears a situation might escalate, they'd said, step away and call for backup. Bob Clary, the park superintendent, had told Stacy the same. Proper protocol, but the man in front of her would think otherwise, see her as fearful.

"Then I'll have to write you a ticket."

The man looked at her now and smiled.

"You're new."

"I've been here four months," Stacy answered.

"Well, Clary's finally hired him a looker. I've always favored brunettes."

"I need your driver's license."

"Sure," he said. "That way you'll know who I am."

The man took out his billfold and handed Stacy the license. Eric Hardaway. She studied the photograph, no beard but recognizable. She filled out the citation, freed the original from the duplicate. When she handed it to Hardaway, he crumpled the paper with his fist, flung it into the water.

"Tell Clary he needs to educate his new hires."

The couple had heard him but stared at their lines, not wishing to get involved. *Afraid.* But Stacy wasn't. What she experienced first when eight years old came again—the sense of entering an expanse where nothing could touch her. Yet this was a different kind of flight, no longer *away from* but *toward*.

Stacy nodded at the stringer staked to the bank.

"How many fish have you got?"

"Don't remember," Hardaway said, his left boot inches from the stringer. "But you might call Clary before you check."

Stacy stepped forward, leaned over to tug the nylon cord. The fish emerged. Hardaway was so close she could smell his muskiness. Stacy counted fourteen and stepped away, began writing the second ticket. Hardaway reeled in and lifted the stringer.

"I'll let you tear up that one," he said, muttering "bitch" as he went up the bank to the trail.

At five Stacy went back to the station, found Clary peering at real estate brochures. Only six weeks from retirement, he spent less time on the trails than in his office sipping coffee and searching for beach property. The three keys to being a good ranger were experience, good manners, and common sense, Clary had told her several times in their four months together, each time with less of an easygoing smile. *Something's wrong with that girl,* Stacy overheard Clary tell a maintenance worker. But she'd known others thought that, why else the years of counselors, therapists, doctors.

Stacy showed him the copies of her citations, told what Hardaway had done.

"He's a real piece of work, ain't he," Clary said, smiling.

"He's a lawbreaker."

"I'd not argue that, and it's put him in jail half a dozen times, including near killing a man in a bar fight. As a matter of fact, I didn't even know he was out."

"What do you want me to do, besides taking these citations to the magistrate?"

"Nothing except throw them in a trash can," Clary answered. "Having to deal with Hardaway isn't worth it for you or me."

"So let him think I'm afraid of him?"

"I'm saying it's best not to provoke him," Clary answered, "the same way you'd not take a stick and poke a rattlesnake. He'll soon do something serious enough to put him back in jail, hopefully for a long time. Whatever that screw-up is, I'd rather it not happen in my park."

"I did my job, and he called me a bitch," Stacy said, "but he knew better than to say it to my face."

"Knew better?" Clary said, grimacing when Stacy nodded.

"And when he comes back?" she asked.

"Look," Clary said. "I'll make this easy for both of us. I'm ordering you not to check Hardaway's license or catch. You keep your ticket pad in your pocket, and remember you're on probation."

The following Wednesday morning the white hatchery truck made its weekly stocking, so Stacy wasn't surprised the lot was crowded with vehicles. By late afternoon many of the stocked fish had been caught, the fishermen gone to await next week's dump. Stacy was about to check the catch-and-release section when she saw Hardaway's blue truck pull into the lot. She watched him walk down the trail, can of corn and rod in his hands. She waited a minute, then followed, stopped at the bridge edge where she could see below but not be seen. Another man, younger, was already fishing the pool. Hardaway sidled up beside him and said something. The other fisherman pulled up his stringer and walked downstream.

Stacy stepped onto the bridge.

"What did you say to that guy?"

"What guy?" Hardaway said.

"Him," Stacy said, nodding downstream.

Hardaway smiled.

"I just told him the fishing's a lot better below this pool."

Stacy stepped off the bridge and walked a few yards into the forest. She pressed a palm against a white oak to steady herself, looked at the brown leaves covering the ground, then the tree trunks, and last the gaps in the greening canopy. *I am a part of only what I see here before me,* she told herself and let go the oak. With her fingers Stacy preened her black hair until she grew calm. She closed her eyes and smelled the woods, went deep inside herself and felt her bones lighten.

Stacy opened her eyes and searched the understory until she found a rock of sufficient size. Then she returned to the bridge. At first, Hardaway ignored Stacy as she watched him from above. She waited until he looked up, then settled her forearm on the bridge railing, the rock filling her hand.

"You ain't going to do that," Hardaway said.

The rock was heavy, but she held it in her palm a few

more moments, then tilted her hand. The rock slipped free and hit the pool's center with a loud splash. She walked off the bridge and up the stream trail, thinking Hardaway might follow but he didn't.

After half a mile she came to where the creek split and followed the narrower branch. The small path ascended. Alongside, the water leapt off rocks to pause in kettled pools. Only brook trout lived here. Unlike the browns and rainbows downstream, Stacy knew these fish were native to these mountains, holdovers from the last ice age. With their orange fins, tiny moons of green, red, and gold brightening their flanks, they were beautiful creatures, but fragile.

Few people came up this far, the path too steep and the air too thin. They'd turn back, out of breath, legs wobbly. But she could make the ascent easily, her body trained to do so. At the beginning of tenth grade, the high school's counselor told her parents that sports might be a way for Stacy to develop better social skills. She chose cross-country, but liked it for reasons opposite of what the adults had hoped. For Stacy, the whole idea was to flee from everyone else. She had been good at that. She ran an extra three miles before school, did workouts alone on Saturday and Sunday. By October she was the fastest on the team. But what mattered were the moments she forgot she had arms and legs, felt instead the gliding sensation of flight, something none of the medications had ever given her. The other girls resented her, especially Stacy's refusal to run with the pack even in practice. By her senior year she was the best cross-country runner in the conference, but one dawn morning she tripped and her Achilles tendon snapped.

The path leveled, a granite outcrop on the right. Here

was her favorite perch. She could see the valley, the stream, even the peaks on the farther mountains. A limb rustled behind her, a glimpse of glossy black feathers. Probably a crow. But at this elevation ravens also could be here.

The name had been bestowed on her last summer at the ranger academy. In nineteenth-century Colorado, the instructor had told them, a woman hoeing in her garden had watched a raven fly toward her, dip low as it passed overhead, and settle a few feet away. The bird performed the same action twice more. Perplexed, the woman looked around the surrounding land. She saw it then, a mountain lion hunched low in the prairie grass. She dropped her hoe and fled, barely reaching the safety of her cabin.

So what have we learned from this story? the instructor had asked. One trainee spoke of the woman's ability, learned from living close to nature, to interpret the bird's actions as a warning. Another spoke of the bird's intelligence, its creation of a way to communicate danger to humans. The instructor waited and Stacy raised her hand for the only time all term. The bird was leading the cougar to prey they could share, she told the instructor. The class was silent but the professor nodded, said Stacy was the first student who'd ever answered correctly.

Later that day, Stacy was in the lunchroom when one trainee nudged another and said, *Look out, here comes the raven.* In the months afterward, Stacy let her dark hair lengthen to cover the sides and back of her neck. She'd had each shoulder tattooed with a feather, though she soon realized such adornment was as unnecessary as the meds that had only helped shackle her.

Flight, but not the sparrow's flight of her childhood,

that vacation morning when her step-uncle took Stacy's small hand and led her into the backyard, then behind the garage. Afterward, the smell of his cigarette lingered on her shorts and shirt, but her parents didn't notice. The next day he took her there again, except this time a sparrow, even at eight she knew the type of bird it was, landed on a nearby tree and began to call to her. Then the bird flew, taking Stacy with it into the sky.

It was Sunday afternoon when Stacy saw Hardaway again, not on the stream but in a BI-LO checkout line. Skoal and Schlitz malt liquor were placed in the plastic bags Hardaway lifted, but an elderly woman took bills from a pocketbook and paid. As the woman accepted her change, he saw Stacy. The old woman said something, and Hardaway, red-faced now, shifted one bag so she could tuck coupons and a receipt inside. As they walked out the glass door to the lot, Stacy wheeled into the checkout lane just vacated, quickly emptied her buggy. When the card reader dinged its acceptance, she told the teenager bagging her groceries she'd be back to get them. Stacy wasn't sure what she was going to do or say, but the truck was already gone when she got outside.

Stacy thought Hardaway might not return to the park, but one morning the blue truck was in the lot. She went to the bridge and saw Hardaway fishing the pool alone. Farther downstream was a middle-aged couple. Stacy checked their license and limits first before returning to the bridge. She watched Hardaway fish.

"Go ahead and write up your fucking tickets," Hardaway muttered.

"I'm not doing that, because I know it wouldn't be you paying the fine, same as it wasn't you paying for those groceries."

Hardaway's face reddened as it had at the store, but not from embarrassment.

"You're going to wish you hadn't said that," he said, raising his eyes to meet hers.

"There's a story I could tell you," Stacy said.

Stacy left the bridge, Hardaway not far behind her. Soon the trail forked. Stacy followed the stream while Hardaway went on to the lot. She walked a ways before she saw the Jeep's owner wading the upper portion of the catch-and-release section, close to where the creek split. A light hatch dimpled the water and he fished a dry. The angler cast well, the fly falling soft on the surface, no line drag. He was catching fish steadily, mainly rainbows but an occasional brown. Each one netted, carefully released. When the angler got to where the creek split, he stepped out of the water.

"That left trib has brook trout in it," she said.

"Not stocked?" he asked.

"Native."

"And it's okay to fish for them?" he asked.

"Yes, and it's not catch-and-release."

The man nodded and went up the tributary to a waterfall. The pool was narrow, rhododendron on both sides, but he made a good cast. The fly was snatched as soon as it touched the surface, the bright colors flashing as the fish was tugged farther downstream into the net.

"You eat that one," Stacy said, as the angler freed the hook. "It's a real fish."

But the man let it go. Stacy turned away in disgust.

She did not return to the parking lot until checkout time. The truck's left front tire had been slashed. She'd expected it would be a tire or windshield. The surveillance camera had also been shattered, pieces of plastic and metal in the grass. Stacy wasn't really surprised, had figured the odds of his doing that fifty-fifty. She took the tire iron from the lockbox and put on the spare.

Clary had left for the day when she returned to the office. Stacy knew that Hardaway would come tomorrow to see her reaction. She went to the storage shed, found an X-ACTO knife and a roll of duct tape, and drove to the cabin. Slashing the tire should be enough to satisfy Hardaway, at least for tonight, but Stacy took the sleeping bag from the closet, set it down in the backyard and got inside. The stars were out, so Stacy lay face up and watched them. After a while she felt the stars coming nearer. They whispered to her. Her sleep was deep and dreamless.

The next morning Stacy waited on the outcrop for Hardaway to come. Soon she saw the blue truck on the park road. She left the ridge, avoiding the trail as she walked to the parking lot. A fly fisherman leaned against his Jeep as he tied on a leader. After he went down the trail, Stacy took the tape and knife and crawled under Hardaway's truck.

Two hours passed before she saw Hardaway sling a stringer of trout in his pickup and drive off.

It was late afternoon when Clary found her checking licenses in the catch-and-release section.

"Hardaway had a wreck. He's in the hospital, pretty banged up but he'll live. Sheriff Patterson thinks he was taking a curve too fast. That's what he thinks, anyway." Clary took a handkerchief from his pocket, patted his brow almost daintily and then put it away. "I saw the duct tape and X-ACTO knife on your truck's dash. Saw what looked and smelled like spilled brake fluid in the lot too. Interesting what the front brakes do when there's a slow leak in the hose. Not that I'm bringing that up to the sheriff though. I don't want the hassle, but when I do your probation evaluation, I'm stating that you repeatedly disobeyed instructions and you shouldn't be kept on. Which might be a blessing if Hardaway figures out what really happened."

He wanted her to react, Stacy knew. They always had—words, tears, something. Clary walked back to the lot and Stacy went upstream, not to check licenses but to be alone on the outcrop. Once there, she gazed at the trees and water below. What humans she saw were so small. The afternoon sun cast her shadow across the outcrop. Stacy raised her arms and saw wings.

# Last Bridge Burned

‡

When the woman had tapped on the locked glass door a few minutes after midnight, she had startled Carlyle. He'd set his broom aside but did not go to the door. Instead, he went around the counter, took the .38 from the shelf under the register. He turned down the radio and looked out the window. The woman was barefoot and had a scrape on her left brow, left forearm scraped also and still bleeding. Though it was October, she wore only frayed jeans and an oversized black T-shirt. Her hair appeared unwashed for days. As she tapped again, he saw a ring adorned with a skull.

*One day you'll learn trouble finds a fellow easy enough without inviting it in.* Carlyle was sixteen when his exasperated father told him that. By the time he'd finally heeded the advice, Carlyle had lost three jobs and two wives. He searched the shadows near the exit ramp for accomplices. Just last week a store one exit down had been robbed. The woman tapped again and Carlyle stepped around the counter, the .38 tucked in the back of his jeans. He stood in front of the door and pointed at the CLOSED sign. When she didn't move, he mouthed the word and turned away.

The outside lights and gas pumps were turned off, the register emptied. He kept the gun tucked in his jeans, picked up the broom and, not looking up, began sweeping his way around the shelves. All that was left was to shut off the radio and inside lights. Then, the woman having given up and gone away, Carlyle could do what he did almost every night before going home, sit a few minutes in the dark on the store's back porch. He'd smoke a cigarette and watch headlights pass below on the interstate. After hours of dealing with people, the soft yellow glow soothed him, as did the sound of the vehicles themselves, a sound like approaching rain.

Now, two years later, the song on the radio brought back that night, and that the woman at the door had not gone away.

*On a late-night east of Nashville*
*My last bridge burned, my money gone*
*The kindness of a stranger*
*Showed me a way to go on.*

By the time he'd finished sweeping, the woman was no longer peering through the glass. Chin down and arms clutched to her chest, she seemed abandoned, much like the dogs dropped off by city folks who'd tired of caring for them. Abandoned cats always found a way to survive, but the dogs stayed close to the exit ramp, waiting.

"What do you want?" he'd asked, after unlocking the door.

"I don't know," the woman finally answered.

Her long hair was stringy and disheveled, her eyes red-veined and glassy. Drunk or drugged, Carlyle knew. She reeked of cigarette smoke and dollar-store perfume.

Younger than he'd thought too, thirty at most, but a hard-lived thirty. She was shivering.

"You don't know?" he asked.

"I was with some people headed to Nashville and they made me get out of the car."

"Why'd they do that?"

"I don't remember," she said, looking toward the exit ramp. "What state am I in?"

*A damn sorry one*, Carlyle thought, then told her North Carolina.

"I was hoping Tennessee."

"That's forty more miles," Carlyle answered. "Those people you were with, you expect they'll come back for you?"

"No, I'd say that bridge is burned."

Carlyle's arm was tiring from holding the door open.

"I guess you can come in for a minute."

"I can't buy anything. I don't have any money."

"I'm not asking you to," he answered, "but I ain't holding this door open but a few seconds longer."

The only light came from a single bulb overhead, but it was enough to find the hydrogen peroxide in the front aisle. Carlyle twisted off the plastic top and handed her the bottle.

"For those scrapes," he told her, and pointed to the bathroom. "There's paper towels and soap in there."

She went to the bathroom. Soon he heard the water running, the squeak of the soap container. In a few minutes the toilet flushed and more water ran in the sink. She came out and handed Carlyle the bottle. Before he could stop her, she eased herself onto the floor, resting her head and back against the wall as she closed her eyes. Her breathing steadied. He spoke to her, said it was time to leave, then shook her shoulder. "Hey, wake up," Carlyle told the woman, but her eyes remained closed. What was he supposed to do now, Carlyle wondered, drag her outside, lock her in for the night, take her home and put her in his house's one bed?

But she'd get the wrong idea, or not think the idea was wrong at all. As disheveled as she looked, there was a prettiness about her, nice enough body inside the shirt and jeans. For a moment Carlyle imagined himself in bed with her. And then what? She'd wake up and find a man almost sixty next to her. She might demand money before leaving. Or worse, not leave and drag him back into the life he'd finally escaped. He could see it all unfold, empty whiskey bottles and late-night dope deals, her needing to *borrow* money before disappearing for days. No, that wasn't going to happen again.

Carlyle went out on the porch, keeping the door open so he'd hear if she woke. A firefly sparked and, as if in reply, he flicked his lighter and lit a cigarette. The cat came out of the weeds, expecting the open tin of sardines he placed nightly on the porch step. Finding none, it disappeared. For three hours Carlyle watched the lights on the interstate, hoping a pair might sweep toward the exit ramp in search of what had been left behind. But the lights never veered.

*You've got a muddy heart* Teresa, his second wife, told him the day she'd left. Afterward, Carlyle wondered if she'd actually said *moody*, but muddy seemed more apt, and the last six years had been an attempt to settle the sediment. Things were getting stirred up again. Carlyle decided to leave the woman where she was and go home, get at least a few hours sleep. He'd write her a note saying the back door was unlocked. If she took a few things, a coffeepot or radio to pawn, a grocery bag of goods, so what. She couldn't haul off a three-hundred-pound safe bolted to the floor. When Carlyle went back into the store, though, her eyes opened. They weren't nearly as glassy and she got to her feet without his help.

"Could I have something to drink?"

"I got water and soft drinks in the cooler," Carlyle answered. "There's coffee too."

"I was thinking something with a bit more kick to it."

"I don't sell alcohol."

"Not even beer?"

Carlyle shook his head.

"Why not?" she asked. "I'd think it would cost you business."

"It cost me a lot more having it around."

"So no bottle of Jim Beam tucked behind the counter?"

"No."

"Coffee then."

Carlyle pushed a cane-back chair toward her and she sat down. He went behind the counter, poured out what remained from the morning, began brewing a fresh pot. *The odor of regret.* That was how he had thought of it for too many mornings.

Carlyle looked out the window and saw a car exiting the ramp. He waited for it to slow and turn in but the car kept going.

"They aren't coming back," she said.

"Is there someone you can call to come get you?" Carlyle asked. "I mean someone else."

She pondered the question, then shook her head.

"Not that would come this far."

"Even family?"

"No."

When the coffee was ready, Carlyle filled a Styrofoam cup, handed it to her. He poured himself a cup.

"Thank you," she said when she'd finished.

She set the empty cup by the chair and closed her eyes again, slouched a bit more in the chair. The radio still played, low but discernible. The news came on, followed by Patsy Cline singing "Crazy." The woman's eyes remained closed, but she softly sang along. She had a good voice.

"That's my theme song," she said, opening her eyes when the song ended.

She seemed to want Carlyle to respond.

"I guess I need to go," she said, and stood up.

"Go where?" Carlyle asked.

"Nashville. I got evicted from my place last week, but that town's like a seesaw. Somebody's always going up if you're going down, so I'll find a place to crash."

"How do you plan to get there?"

"Walk down to the interstate and hold out my thumb."

"Barefoot?"

"I got here that way."

Carlyle looked at the front door as if it might open and, like a rewinding movie, the woman would backstep out the door and all the way to the car and keep going. But life didn't work that way.

"There's a bus station in Asheville," Carlyle said. "I'll take you there."

"I don't have money for the ticket."

"I'll buy it."

For the first time, she looked at him suspiciously.

"What do you expect in return?"

"Nothing."

"Nothing?"

"Look," Carlyle answered. "You can hitchhike or walk or take the bus. It don't matter to me, but if it's the bus we leave now."

"Okay," she said.

Carlyle went down the aisle nearest the door. Amid a shelf thick with ball caps and sunglasses he unearthed a pair of green flip-flops.

"Here," he said, then took some bills from the safe.

They drove east on I-40. The woman closed her eyes and leaned her head against the window. The silence and darkness helped him pretend she wasn't in the cab. It wasn't even about her particularly, just being so close to a woman that his hand could touch her hair, her face, her body. There were women who came into the store and flirted. The only relapse he'd had in four years was because of one of them. Not nearly as young as the woman beside him, in her late forties. She was a drinker but Carlyle had thought, wrongly, that he could handle that.

The sun was rising as they drove into Asheville. The bus station was in the part of town the tourists didn't visit. A woman in an overcoat and sweatpants slept on a wooden bench. On the next block a man gave a nod as the truck approached, stepped back from the curb when Carlyle didn't slow. The space under the awning was vacant so Carlyle pulled up close to the door. He put the truck in neutral and told her to find out the price of the ticket. She came back out and told him forty-eight dollars. He took out three twenties, held them out the window.

"I guess you want me to promise I won't spend this on drugs and liquor instead," she said as she took the bills.

"It's yours now so you decide what to do with it. I'm tired and I'm going home."

But she didn't leave.

"I ain't giving you more money."

"It's not that," she said.

"What then?"

"Getting sober," she asked. "Any advice?"

"A person who never took advice himself ought not give it," Carlyle said. "You'll decide to keep drinking or stop on your own."

"Fair enough," she said. "I never did get your name. Mine's Sabrina."

"You better get on inside," Carlyle said.

"All right," she said, "and thank you."

Carlyle drove off without a glance in the rearview mirror. When he got back to his house he was too restless to sleep. He made some coffee and sat in the front room, staring at nail holes in the wall where pictures once hung. Then he drove to the store.

That was two years ago. Carlyle had not made the connection until he heard the name and lyrics on the radio. A Google search on a library computer confirmed it. The same face but more filled out, healthier. Carlyle read a couple of articles about her, how she was sober and loving life again, the usual AA stuff about hitting rock bottom and needing a higher power. Now she and her song were certain to get CMA nominations, perhaps even one for a Grammy. The seesaw had tilted.

But that was her life, not his, Carlyle reminded himself that evening as he set the open tin of sardines on the porch step. His heart was settled. No ups, no downs. Be grateful for that, he told himself. The cat came out from under the porch and began to eat as Carlyle watched the headlights tunnel into the night.

# Ransom

Later, Jennifer would recall how she and her friends joked that the campus was a place where people often weren't what they appeared to be. The woman in slippers muttering to herself could be a homeless person or an acclaimed historian, the wild-haired fellow in a flowing white coat a psych ward escapee or Nobel Laureate. So that evening when she left the rec center to meet friends in town, Jennifer wasn't overly wary of the man approaching from the other direction. He wore an ill-fitting rumpled suit, his hair needing a comb, his face a razor. Had she been with Mary or Abigail, they might have made amusing guesses about which department he belonged to.

The man stopped a few yards before her and smiled. She was about to say "Sorry, I don't have any change," but he spoke first.

"Jennifer, correct?" When she didn't respond, he waved a hand as if to dismiss any confusion. "I know your father."

Although the accent was southern, there was a formality in his tone. Her father had connections with people all over the country, especially here at the university, where he was a distinguished alumnus and prominent donor.

"Yes," she answered.

The man stepped closer, right hand outstretched. She shifted her cell phone from her right to left hand. Better this than some creepy attempt at a hug, she thought, then saw his hand held a handkerchief.

Jennifer awoke to fierce pain, as if something was trying to tear her right arm from her body. Then the jolts lessened and she opened her eyes. Only darkness and the sense of movement. Another big bump made her head swirl with yellow sparks. When the pain dimmed, she shifted so her shoulder wasn't pinned beneath her. Every few seconds Jennifer felt a buffeting of air as a vehicle passed from the opposite direction. She moved her legs and touched metal, below and to the side. Not a van, Jennifer thought, a car trunk. *Never walk alone*, her parents had warned her, as had the counselors at freshman orientation. She always returned to campus with a group, but sometimes, like tonight, coming directly from Pilates, she had to walk into town alone. Jennifer felt in her tunic for the cell phone and pepper spray. Both gone.

She must have lost consciousness again, for when a jolt awoke her, they seemed to be on a different road, bumpier, fewer vehicles rushing past. The road dipped and rose, causing her body to shift and the pain to flare. Jennifer reminded herself people were searching for her. Many people, because her parents and the university would make certain of it. Surely someone saw what happened, or a surveillance camera filmed it. The vehicle, maybe even the license plate number, would already be known. There would be roadblocks, police cars on the lookout. Be glad he hasn't stopped, Jennifer told herself. As long as he's moving, you're safe.

The road smoothed again. Traffic increased. A police siren wailed by but the car did not slow and return. Drained, she drifted into a twilight sleep. She might have dreamed, but a bump erased its contents. Jennifer was thirsty and wondered how many hours had passed. Two, six? The more hours, surely the better. She tried to focus on what to do when the car stopped, but the pain kept interrupting. After a while, gravel crunched under the tires. The car made a final swaying descent and halted.

The driver's-side door opened and shut. Her left hand searched for something weighty and solid. *Tire iron.* The term came to her, though Jennifer wasn't sure what one was. But there was nothing more than a blanket. An absurd idea came to her of throwing the blanket over the man. Instead, she folded her legs. Kick and then run. The trunk opened and a flashlight glared.

The man did not grab for her but took a step back, almost deferentially.

"I know your shoulder and ankle are hurt, Jennifer, but otherwise, are you okay?"

She didn't answer.

"This isn't about harming you," he said. "I've kidnapped you, and once the ransom is paid, you'll be set free. I'll make you as comfortable as I can. Your parents will pay and then it will be done. Okay?"

"Yes," Jennifer said, wanting to believe it was true.

"I don't want to chloroform you again. Your shoulder's hurt so I'll let you get yourself most of the way out, but please don't try anything. We're miles from another house, and if you got lost in these woods you would be in real trouble. You understand?"

"Yes."

"All right then."

Jennifer could think of no reason to fight getting out, and the thought of the arm being jerked made her stomach tighten. She used her good arm and swung her legs over. Her ankle gave way and she'd have fallen if he hadn't helped her.

"Just stand here a minute so your head can clear," he said.

A bird called from a nearby tree and Jennifer realized much of the darkness came from the forest's canopy. *Run,* she told herself, but as she tensed her legs to turn, the man's hand clasped her left arm. He pointed the flashlight at a small cabin. Beside the porch, a metal sign read FOR RENT: WEEKLY OR MONTHLY RATES.

He helped her up the steps. The door was unlocked, a glass pane above the doorknob broken. Inside, the front room was sparsely furnished—a table, a few chairs, a couch, to the right a small kitchen. Nothing suggested recent habitation.

"There's the bathroom if you need it," the man said, pointing to a door in the narrow hallway.

Jennifer went in and shut the door. The lock had been removed. Besides the commode, sink, and medicine cabinet, there was a cramped tiled shower. She tried to think of something she could do, some weapon or ploy, but her right arm was useless, her mind hazy. When she came out, the man led her downstairs to a small, windowless room whose pale light came from a single string-drawn bulb. An air mattress lay on the floor, on it a pillow and neatly folded blankets and sheets. Next to them were a sweatshirt and string-tied sweatpants like those her father wore on weekend mornings, an outfit Jennifer and her mother often joked about. There was a chair and a card table, and on the table magazines and paperbacks in neat stacks. Everything seemed placed with considerable care, as if awaiting a guest more than a captive.

"I know it's not very much, but once the ransom's paid you'll be back home."

"But where are we now?"

"North Carolina."

The man lingered in the doorway. A few years older than her father, she guessed, but also bigger than her father, stronger-looking.

"My parents and my little sister will be worried," Jennifer said, having read that you needed to build empathy and thus be seen as a fellow human. "My little sister's name is Linda. She's only eleven."

"I know they're worried," the man answered.

"Something's torn in my shoulder. I need to see a doctor."

"That's why we'll get this done as quickly as possible, but it could take a while."

"Let me call them on my cell phone, or your cell phone. That way my parents will know I'm all right and you'll get your money quicker. Just tell me how much you want. My parents will pay it and they won't call the police, if I tell them not to."

"Your cell phone's where you dropped it, but I'm certain the police have contacted your parents by now," the man answered. "That's why this has to be done slower than you or me would favor. I'll bring you some food directly. If you need to use the bathroom again, it's that bucket in the corner. I'm sorry, but that's the way it has to be."

"Please," Jennifer said, tearing up. "I'm really hurting."

"I'll bring you food and water," he said, "and something for the pain."

The man left. During last September's media frenzy, Jennifer's father had warned her that his prominence might cause some harassment at the university despite, or even because of, the endowment he'd made to the school's fine arts center. But he'd never warned her about something like this. She had friends in prep school and at the university who came from families with similar wealth. Not one of them had ever said a word about being kidnapped for ransom. After all, this wasn't South America. UV rays, credit card fraud, opening email attachments—those they'd been warned about. Jennifer gave her right shoulder the slightest shrug and winced. Something was torn, which meant no Pilates for weeks, maybe months. She'd have to be even more diligent about her weight. Also her classes. What if she missed so many she'd lose a whole semester? *You're locked in a basement and could be tortured, raped, murdered, and you're worried about fucking Pilates?* she thought. *This is real. You think those bodies they find in ditches and woods are just some illusion?*

Jennifer tried to turn the doorknob with her left hand. It was locked. No windows. Her breaths grew rapid, but no air seemed to reach her lungs. She had been left inside this cinderblock tomb to slowly smother to death.

*You're being ransomed*, Jennifer told herself. *Ransomed.*
This wasn't about hurting her. It was about money, and her
family had plenty of that. Ransom, she whispered, repeat-
ing the word's soft consonants until her breaths slowed.
She and her parents had argued often, exchanged plenty
of harsh words, but they did love her and would pay any
price, even millions, to get her back safe. Her father would
know exactly what to do. Though her breaths steadied, Jennifer's hands still trembled, and she could not stop them
from doing so.

The man returned with a bottle of water and a white
paper bag. She smelled the grease that spotted the paper.
He took out the food and unwrapped it. Soggy bread, some
kind of meat stuffed inside.

"Take these," he said, handing her two aspirin-sized
tablets.

"What is it," she asked.

"For pain."

"How do I know that?"

"Look and you'll see who made it," the man said, showing her the drug name on the bottle. "That certainly should
assure you it's safe."

Jennifer placed the tablets in her mouth and swallowed
them. The man stepped back and leaned against the wall,
nodded for her to sit at the table.

"How do you know so much about my family and me?"

He smiled.

"We have the Internet down here too. A few of us even
know how to use it."

Jennifer felt her face redden.

"I didn't mean it that way."

"You better eat that food while it's warm."

Jennifer took a bite. How many hours had passed since lunch? She ate the first hamburger, then, after a few moments of hesitation, decided to eat the second. The food nestled in her stomach, and Jennifer was overcome with a drowsy satiety rarely felt since tenth grade. She'd drunk all of the water, so he went upstairs and got another bottle. He twisted off the cap and placed it on the table.

"Thank you," she said, lifting it with her left hand as he went to stand by the door.

He had taken off the coat. His white shirt, though wrinkled, was clean, the shoes worn but polished. He hadn't shaved in a few days, but he didn't have the musty odor of the homeless. His voice was calm, sane. *Build a bond. Build a bond.*

"You know my name, but what is yours?"

"Jim will do."

"Jim?"

"Yes."

"Do you have a family, Jim?"

"A son who lives out of state."

"And a wife?" Jennifer asked, nodding at the gold band on his hand.

"She died a while back."

"I'm sorry to hear that."

"In a lot of ways it was a relief for her," Jim said. "We had a daughter, but she died too."

It was a connection, but Jennifer wasn't sure how to manage it.

"Was she about my age?"

"A few years older."

"That must have been hard."

"No need to talk about it," Jim said. "It's done."

"I understand," Jennifer said carefully, "but you can understand how my parents are feeling right now."

"Yes, I believe I can."

He came to the table and took the wrappers and bag but left the bottled water.

"I'll be back in a few hours," he said. "Those magazines and books, they might help you pass the time."

After he left, Jennifer removed the baking tray covering the metal bucket. It wasn't easy or comfortable but she managed to empty her bladder, place the tray back over the bucket. She didn't feel as humiliated as she thought she would. It was even a bit funny. Jennifer felt calmer as she lay down on the mattress. She'd be rescued soon, she really would. Jennifer gingerly moved her shoulder and found the pain had dimmed. Her jeggings and tunic reeked of grime and car exhaust, so she changed into the sweat clothes. Jennifer closed her eyes and slept.

There was no clock, but three meals meant a day had passed. He brought her food and, with each meal, more tablets for the pain. On the third day he let her take a shower. While the water ran, Jennifer searched but could find no weapon, not even a rusty razor blade. To break the mirror and wield a glass shard wouldn't work. Woozy from the drug and left-handed, what chance would she have? She did think of something else though.

"If I give you my username and password, could you at least send my parents an email to show I'm safe?"

"Do you really think I'd fall for that?" he asked.

"No," Jennifer answered softly. "But I've got to try, don't I? If your daughter were in my place, you'd want her to try, wouldn't you?"

"I think she did try," he answered.

Hours later, when Jim returned with the food and tablets, Jennifer told him the shoulder hurt less and she didn't need the pills.

"You have to take them," he told her. "I can force you to, but I hope it won't come to that."

She took them. He made her open her mouth and lift her tongue to be certain.

When counting meals became too tedious to keep up with, two showers meant a week had passed. Jennifer realized, with a sense of relief, that time didn't matter. Food and water were provided before they were missed, as were the clean sweatshirt and sweatpants, undergarments, sanitary napkins. The pills helped, and she did not resist them, even took more when offered. When Jennifer looked in the bathroom mirror, she saw prominent cheekbones, a tautness to her upper neck and chin. She slid a hand over her tightening abdomen. Jennifer thought of the Pilates class that had caused her to be alone the evening of her abduction. A seven p.m. weekend session for, as the flyer said, those with weight-management issues. The svelte, spandex-encased instructor always seemed either amused or irritated as she barked instructions. The studio was an octagon walled with mirrors. One of the most overweight girls called it *the corral.*

Now, as she stared into the cabin's bathroom mirror, Jennifer thought how much easier things would have been if her father had brought home product samples. No exercise regimens, no points calculated, no stepping on scales to watch the red line shiver, then pronounce its judgment. The results might have even inspired a new ad campaign: *Be pain-free and lose weight at the same time.*

Jim knocked on the door, asked if Jennifer was all right.

"Just admiring myself," she answered.

As he followed her downstairs, Jennifer asked why the ransom hadn't been paid yet.

"Things like this take time," he answered.

A thought came as she settled on the mattress.

"If it isn't paid, will I die, Jim?"

"We all die," he answered.

"I mean die here."

"You don't need to be worrying about that," he said, then nodded at the magazines. "You want me to get you some new ones?"

"No," Jennifer answered. "They'd be as boring as these are."

Jim brought her a radio, a device as antiquated to her as a sextant. It picked up news stations, but soon Jennifer left the dial on the easy-listening channel. It was better than an iPod—no downloading the songs she liked or songs people expected her to like. This music *was* easy, soft and soothing and always there, requiring nothing, not even being listened to.

One day Jennifer faked taking the tablets, slid them into a pocket. But a while later after Jim left, she began to feel anxious so swallowed them. She lay on the mattress, mostly easing in and out of sleep. One of her professors had ranted about the tyranny of technology and Jennifer realized he was right. The nag of her cell phone, every call, email, text, no matter how trivial, demanded a response. Nags and gnats. The same thing, she thought, remembering the grainy clouds that drove her inside at her family's summer house. An unceasing swirl of demands, hadn't that been her whole life?

She and Jim didn't talk much, but she found out a few things about him. He'd owned a small business but lost it in the recession. His wife had been an office manager at the county extension office. One day Jennifer asked how his daughter had died, but Jim didn't answer except to say that his son had the sense to leave this place at eighteen, or he'd likely be dead too. Jennifer asked if Jim had any hobbies. He knitted his brow and seemed to give the question a good deal of thought.

"No," he finally answered. "I guess I'm past that sort of thing."

When Jennifer asked about the ransom, Jim told her that negotiations were moving along. Soon, he promised. She occasionally thought of escape, but what was the point if it would soon be over? Jim hadn't hurt her, never threatened to. She wasn't afraid of him, not really. If the negotiations took so long, she suspected her parents were to blame.

Except for her freedom and a cell phone, he gave her what she requested: candy, soft drinks, more pills more often. She tired of reading and asked for a television. Though it picked up only three channels, that was enough. Jennifer liked game shows, especially when contestants dressed in silly costumes, hoping to win a dishwasher or an oriental rug. At first, she enjoyed hearing the cheery voices, but then she tired of them, choosing the radio's soothing music instead. Silenced, the tiny people inside the glass seemed like fish in an aquarium.

Then a morning came when, as Jim took her upstairs for a shower, he told her she'd been in the cellar for thirty days. Jennifer couldn't tell if it seemed longer or shorter than that. After toweling off, she studied her face and shoulders, raised her arms and examined them too. Her face could never be beautiful—forehead a bit too broad, eyes set a bit too close—but otherwise she resembled the slim women, breathing mannequins as she'd thought of them, who filled the glossy pages of high-fashion magazines her mother read.

Jennifer widened her mouth to see her teeth. Her parents and dentist acted like one day without flossing would cause her teeth to spill out like a snapped strand of beads. Watching herself in the mirror, Jennifer raised a finger, tapped the nail against her front teeth. They were all still there, if a bit gray.

She'd dressed and they'd gone back down the stairs. Jim told her that very soon they would trade places and Jennifer would be the one free. I'm sorry you had to be involved, he said, but it was the only way. He took out his billfold and showed her a black-and-white photograph of his daughter.

When she awoke the next morning, the door was open. Beside the bed were the jeggings and tunic, her cell phone and Kavu bag. On the table were an orange-tinted prescription bottle and a neatly printed note—RANSOM PAID. Jennifer placed the bottle and phone in the Kavu bag and made her way up the steps to the main floor. The front room was unchanged. Nothing on the counters, chairs pressed close to the dining table, trash cans empty. Jennifer looked out the front window. No vehicle, just a dirt drive that led up a hill into the woods. The front door was unlocked. She took a glass from the cupboard and went to the faucet. She drank, then leaned and splashed water on her face, trying to emerge from the dreamy state she'd been in for, how long had it been? Jim had told her yesterday but the number escaped her.

Some muted but insistent inner alarm told her to flee now, that Jim might change his mind and return, so Jennifer went down the steps and into the yard. Despite the trees the sunlight was harsh, so much so that Jennifer stepped back onto the porch. She took out the prescription bottle and went back inside for more water. After a few minutes she came out again, slowly walked up the drive and soon came to a dirt road. The cell phone had been charged and she had a signal. Thirty minutes later a silver North Carolina Highway Patrol car appeared.

After the arrest and a week of cameras and microphones; after a trial that brought more cameras and microphones, along with questions of individual guilt and corporate culpability; after James Dillard received a verdict of guilty and a sentence of twenty years in prison; after Jennifer's second involuntary stay at a drug-treatment clinic, Jennifer's parents accepted that she'd have to be the one to alter her life. They threatened to take her credit cards away until she mentioned that a solicitation arrest would bring yet another round of cameras and microphones, and more uncomfortable questions about James Dillard and the source of his daughter's addiction.

The credit cards were returned and Jennifer found an apartment in a neighborhood gentrified enough to support a dealer who made home deliveries. Once a month, Jennifer took the bus to the prison. She and Jim sat across from each other, Plexiglas between them. It would be for only a few minutes and wasn't so different than when they had been in North Carolina except, sometimes, they spoke about his daughter.

# The Belt

The rain announced itself timidly, a few soft taps on the tin roof. Soon the rain fell steadily. Since it was July, Jubal waited for rumbles of thunder, the dark sky darkening more as lightning stabbed the ridges. Then rain would gallop down, pounding the tin before the sun herded the storm into Tennessee. But this was more like November rain, the kind that lingered days. Night came and the rain continued. As Jubal settled into the shuck mattress to sleep, it hit the roof not like hooves but a drummer boy's quickstep. When he awoke the next morning, the sound overhead was the same martial cadence, so he was not surprised that he'd dreamed again of the war, of the moments after his horse buckled and he'd been thrown. As Jubal rose from the bed, the aches of eight decades awakened too. His bones always hurt more in wet weather so before dressing he rubbed liniment on his back and shoulders. He looked out the window at the rain, the rivulets coursing down the ridge. As he pressed the brass buckle into the belt holes, he felt the familiar indention the minié ball had made.

Jubal went into the kitchen and unhinged the range's iron door, struck a match to the wood and newspaper he'd tindered the night before. He set the coffeepot on the iron eye. The house was chilly, so for the first time in two months he made a hearth fire, stood in front of it hands out until the coffeepot heated. He filled his cup and stepped onto the front porch and stared across the pasture at the French Broad. Water usually clear enough to see the river's bottom was now brown as his coffee. The sandbars had disappeared, but the big boulder midstream broke the onrushing water like a ship's hull. No flood had ever submerged this rock.

When Jubal saw the buggy coming up the muddy lane, he remembered it was Saturday. Rob, his grandson, was bringing the boy to stay with him while Rob and his wife, Lizzie, went to Marshall. Rob pulled up beside the porch and Lizzie and the child got out, Lizzie holding an umbrella over their heads as they came up the steps. Rob pulled the brake and brought the canvas tote sack onto the porch.

"Clear most all week and now it comes a-pouring," Lizzie said, shaking her head.

"It's surely over the banks down in the bottomland," Rob said, as the three of them stared at the river. "They's likely crops being washed away."

"You sure you ought to go?" Jubal asked.

"I checked and the bridge is fine," Rob said.

"For now," Jubal cautioned, "but if it don't clear by afternoon it may not be."

"The eggs and butter won't keep till next market day," Lizzie said, "and you know we got need of cash money."

"I know that," Jubal said. "I just want you all to be careful."

"If that bridge looks chancy on the way back," Rob said, "we'll stay with Lizzie's folks."

"If it comes to that, would you mind keeping the boy till morning?" Lizzie asked.

"Of course not," Jubal said, taking the child into his arms and nuzzling him with his beard. "Me and him will be fine, won't we, partner?"

The child giggled and clung tighter around Jubal's neck.

"We best get on," Lizzie said, bussing the boy on the cheek. "You be sweet and maybe we'll bring you back a play-pretty."

"Rub that lucky buckle of yours," Rob said as he released the brake. "Maybe it'll settle this weather down."

Rob jerked the reins and the wagon went down the pike toward the bridge. Jubal shifted the child to one arm.

"Let's get you out of this nasty weather," he said, giving a last look at the river. The boulder was still visible, but less of it showed.

Once inside, Jubal set the boy and the sack on the davenport. He went to the back porch and brought the box filled with the whirligigs and animals he'd carved for the child. He set the toys between the davenport and the hearth.

"There you are, Jubal," he told his namesake, and seated the boy on the floor. He poured himself another cup of coffee and watched the child play. A lucky man, he'd often said of himself, and worn the source of that luck every day since the afternoon it saved his life. He had never meant it as a provocation, but in the first years after the war the buckle's etched eagle, wings and talons extended, had caused hard stares, at times words, and once a fistfight.

Now only a handful of veterans remained. There was another war, bigger than any before, and despite what

President Wilson said the country was edging into it. Jubal feared that Rob, his only grandson, might be called up. He almost expected it. Lucky as Jubal had been, little good fortune had found its way to those around him. *Pure luck,* his comrades called it as they'd marveled at the buckle and its indention. After Chickamauga, some touched the buckle before battle, but it seemed the luck was indeed pure, unable to be diluted and spread to others, then or afterward. Jubal's wife and son and daughter were all shadowed by stones now. Rob, his only grandchild, had found little luck in his life. He'd married well, but he and Lizzie had encountered a passel of troubles. Their barn had burned three Octobers ago, a year's worth of curing tobacco lost, but before that two miscarriages had sent Lizzie into a dark place.

But luck had come with this child playing before him. Despite his being born a month too soon and puny, the boy not only survived but quickly grew hale and hearty. Jubal had never asked, but he'd always wondered if Rob and Lizzie thought naming the child after him would help the boy survive. The Franklin clock chimed, another hour passing with no sign of the rain easing. He went to the window, but the glass was too streaked to see much. The child got up, gained his balance, toddled over to Jubal, and raised his arms to be lifted.

"Getting hungry, are you?" Jubal said, picking up the boy.

He felt the hippin. It was dry so he set the child down and opened the sack. He got the nursing bottle, put on his coat and hat, and went out the back door to the springhouse. By the time he got back, the hat and coat were soaked. The child suckled the rubber tip until nothing was left, then put his head on Jubal's chest and closed his eyes. Jubal walked to the back room and laid the boy on the bed. He poured another cup of coffee and went onto the front porch. The boulder was only a foot or so above the water. The pike and the lower pasture had vanished except for the barbed-wire fence. He thought of Rob and Lizzie and hoped they had the good sense to stay in Marshall. Even if the bridge held, the pike could be washed out.

Jubal realized he had not eaten, so went to the larder and got the cornbread. To crumble it into a glass of buttermilk would be all the better, but the hat and coat he'd set by the hearth weren't ready for another trip to the springhouse. He slathered the bread with blackberry jam and ate it before swallowing the last of the coffee. Jubal checked on the child and went back onto the porch. The boulder was gone. Where it had been, the water appeared smooth, almost calm, that illusion holding until driftwood and trees swept past, then a chicken coop and a flatboat that slowly twirled as if searching for the river it had once known.

The fence was gone now and so was most of the pasture. The cow and its calf huddled in the upper corner. More things once alive sped by—chickens and dogs, livestock, then a body. It swept past so quickly Jubal could do nothing but stare. Holding an old field jacket over his head, he crossed the soaked ground. He opened the latch-gate and herded the cow and calf out. Back on the porch, Jubal saw what was more a portent than the one body. A barn lay on its side, drifting down the valley like an overturned ark.

He had built this house himself. Jubal knew it was solid, but what held it to the earth were flat creek rocks and four locust beams. No one lived close by except Rob and Lizzie, and their house was closer to the river than this one, so the only shelter was here. He went to the back room and sat beside the child. "You been lucky once," Jubal told the boy softly. As if evoking a talisman for the both of them, Jubal thought again of Chickamauga, that moment in the cavalry skirmish when his horse buckled and hurled him to the ground. He had rolled onto his back just as the enemy cavalryman slowed his mount and leaned toward Jubal, the pistol's muzzle only feet away. Jubal did not hear the shot but saw the flash and then smoke from the charge. The man rode on as Jubal waited for the pain, and what would surely relieve it. He'd placed an open palm beneath his shirt and slid it slowly down his stomach, then under the belt and trousers. No blood or torn flesh. Some sort of misfire, he'd concluded, rising to his feet. The battle had moved on, leaving dead men and horses scattered around him. Only then had Jubal looked for a tear in his jacket, saw instead the indention where the minié ball had struck the brass buckle.

Jubal listened for a few moments and noticed a change in the rain's cadence. He placed a hand on the boy's hair and stroked it. The child shifted a bit, but his eyes did not open. Jubal stepped out on the porch and found the rain was indeed slackening. To the east, the sky had begun paling. But too late. The pasture was under the river now. Jubal watched a rattlesnake attempt to swim across the current, fail to make the porch steps only yards away. A hog pen swept by, the hog itself roiling behind it. It's got to crest soon, he told himself, but the water had reached the first step and begun seeping under the house. Crying came from the back room, so Jubal went inside and lifted the child into his arms, felt the hippin.

"Best keep it that way, boy," Jubal told the child. "It might be the onliest thing dry on you soon."

They went to the front porch. The rain had almost stopped but water continued thickening around the steps. Soon it would be all the way under the house. Jubal went back inside and changed his shoes for boots. He got the child out of his gown and into his rompers, wrapped him in the blanket, and went to the back porch. There was nowhere to go except up the ridge, but after he'd gained a few yards of ground Jubal slipped, turning onto his side to protect the child. He slid almost to the back steps before stopping. For a moment he lay there, breathing hard as the child squalled in his arms. Something had twisted or torn in his knee, so first he kneeled, then slowly got to his feet. The brown floodwater reached all the way to the ridge now, and Jubal knew they wouldn't survive another slide, so he sloshed through the water to where mountain laurel grew. He did not try to stand but got on his knees, holding the child in one arm as he worked his way upward. One plant pulled free of the earth, but he caught hold of another before they started to slide.

When there was no more laurel, he stopped. Jubal's heart banged so hard against his chest the ribs felt like a rickety fence about to shatter. If it's lasted eighty-one years it can last a few more minutes, he told himself, and tried to figure out what to do next. He patted the child through the blanket. A few yards above them was a stand of tulip poplars. Though their branches were too high to grasp, a trunk to grab hold of might be enough to keep them alive.

Jubal did not look back because he did not need to. He could hear the water rising behind them. The child was silent now, as if he too listened. Then came a loud rending as the house pulled free of its moorings. Jubal's heart continued to hammer and his knee burned. Between the poplars and the laurel was a scrub oak. He stabbed his free hand deep into the soggy ground and pulled closer. Only then did he see what coiled around it. This snake wasn't as large as the one he'd watched earlier from the front porch, but it had the same triangular head and blunt tail.

"I just want to share it with you a minute," Jubal said softly. "Then me and this chap will be on our way."

Jubal slowly grasped the sapling inches above the snake, but as he pulled himself closer his hand slipped downward, pressed the snake's cold scales. Its muscles tensed and then contracted tighter around the trunk. The rattle buzzed twice, ceased. Neither of them moved until Jubal felt the water rising onto his boots. "Git on, now," he told the snake, and pressed his hand slowly but firmly on its body. The snake gave a brief rattle, then unspooled and slithered past them into the water. Jubal pulled himself even with the scrub oak. He was so tired, so old. The river whispered for him to surrender. Everything else has, the water said. Jubal pushed ahead and reached his free arm around the closest poplar. He looked up at the branches, the nearest thirty feet above him. Even if he could have gone on, there was nothing farther up the ridge to hold on to. Beyond the branches was only a too-late clearing sky. He looked back. All he could see was water.

Jubal touched the buckle.

"Be lucky one more time," he told it.


They found him late the next morning. The sun was out and something flashed from within a stand of poplars. Some kind of signal, the two men in the flatboat thought, and lifted their oars and made their way across the drowned farm. At first they thought it an apparition caused by fatigue, because the child seemed to be hovering above the water. Then they saw the belt around the tree trunk, heard a soft whimpering, and they marveled at a child held aloft and alive in the grasp of an eagle.

# In the Valley

✠

When Serena Pemberton stepped out of the Commodore seaplane in July of 1931, a small but fervent contingent of reporters and photographers awaited her. Except for the pilot, she was alone. Those who would accompany her to the logging camp, both beast and human, had arrived by ship the night before. They were already on the train that would take them from Miami to North Carolina. All except for her minion Galloway, who'd procured an automobile to drive Serena to the station. As the metal ramp was readied, Galloway positioned himself beside the bottom step. He was short and wiry, shabbily dressed, a purple stump protruding from one sleeve. As cameras flashed mere inches from his face, he did not blink.

As Serena descended, the first question shouted at her addressed the rumors surrounding her husband's death. For a moment, it didn't appear she would answer, but when her booted feet settled securely on the ground, the question was asked again, but with a caveat, had she loved her husband?

"I loved my husband, but one always learns from disappointments."

"But what of his death, Mrs. Pemberton, and what of so many others of your acquaintance?" the reporter asked.

"Logging is a dangerous business," she answered.

Galloway was in front of her now, but Serena, almost a head taller, was clearly visible. He cleared a path as more questions came:

Would she continue to fight against the national park, and would she address the rumor that she was connected to the recent demise of Horace Kephart, the park's chief advocate?

Did she oppose the Davis-Bacon Act?

Why risk a trans-Atlantic enterprise when she and her late husband had achieved so much in the States?

Galloway opened the DeSoto's passenger door. Serena was about to get in when the sole woman in the group, a reporter for *The New Republic*, stepped close. She was very young but, like Serena, tall and blond.

"When will you have achieved all your ambitions, Mrs. Pemberton?" she asked, as others jostled around them.

"When the world and my will are one," Serena answered.

# 1

Ross saw the eagle first. He was about to resume work but instead leaned his ax handle against a tulip poplar, tucked his hands in the back pockets of his overalls, and watched the bird glide above the valley floor. The rest of the crew soon saw the eagle too. Henryson stopped rolling his midmorning cigarette. Snipes lowered his newspaper and set down a last bite of biscuit. Having noticed the silence of his fellows, Quince opened his eyes and gazed drowsily upward. The eagle came toward the lower ridge, its shadow rippling over the slash and stumps the crew had left the previous day. Then the shadow paused. The eagle tucked its wings and javelined earthward. At the last moment, the wings fanned, talons stretching to seize and crush a rattle-snake's head. The men watched as the snake's body flogged the ground, its rattle winding down to a last feeble twitch. At the sound of a metal whistle, raptor and serpent rose as one, as though the reptile's body were revived and sudden-winged, evoking the fire-drakes of Albion.

"She's back," Snipes said, as the men followed the bird's flight toward the head of the valley. There they saw their employer of three years, a woman who at first had done things no woman they'd ever known would have dared, then later no man. As on that first morning when her now-deceased husband introduced her at the Cataloochee camp, Serena Pemberton was astride the white Arabian, rare and imperious as its owner. Those 34,000 acres having been logged, the operation had moved to this 7,000-acre tract, the last of her North American holdings. In November, shortly after her husband's death, she'd left for Brazil, leaving the bookkeeper Meeks with instructions that the job be finished by midnight on the last day in July. Now it was July 28 and she had returned.

The crew watched as Serena swung the lure like a lariat. The eagle descended and landed beside the horse. It released the rattlesnake and took the offered hank of meat. Galloway, dagger in hand, knelt beside the reptile. He made a single swipe, then pocketed the rattle. The eagle lifted again and settled on Serena's leather gauntlet. Horse, eagle, and rider disappeared into an outbuilding that had previously served as a garage for Meeks's Pierce-Arrow. Galloway followed. The valley's ridges, which for an hour had been a cacophony of axes, saws, and falling trees, were silent as the other crews also watched. When Serena and Galloway came out of the stable, two burly newcomers in dark suits lifted a steamer trunk from a boxcar, then hauled it to the two-bedroom A-frame that had served as Meeks's living quarters. As the men took the trunk inside, Serena and Galloway went and stood on the business office's porch.

Quince, the fourth member of Snipe's crew, was a recent hire. He had logged twelve years in the swampy lowlands of Georgia, working among men he'd believed world-class liars with their tales of cottonmouth moccasins thick enough to clog stovepipes, alligators long as cabooses, all manner of haints and spectrals and catawampuses. But he'd found these highlanders outlied all comers. For a month he'd been told about Serena Pemberton: how she rode a horse and swung an ax like a man and how anyone who crossed her—partner, competitor, lawman, worker, husband—was good as dead. Quince had heard about Galloway also, the one-handed man who shadowed the woman and did much of the killing. The henchman had even tried to murder George Pemberton's bastard child and the mountain girl who'd birthed it, aided by his mother, who, despite being blind and almost motionless, guided Galloway to his fleeing victims. The old crone could see into the future, Snipes's crew had said, even prophesying that her son and Mrs. Pemberton could not die separately. *Like it wouldn't be hard enough just to kill one of them,* Henryson had said.

Quince had listened indulgently to these and other wild tales and superstitions, most of which came from the crew foreman Snipes, whose bell-dangling haberdashery, like his clothing's varied-hued patches, Quince had seen before only on playing cards. The other crew members had, albeit to a lesser degree, adopted their foreman's belief that bright colors warded off a host of dangers, even lightning strikes. Quince had disputed nothing until Snipes made the most outrageous claim of all, that Mrs. Pemberton had trained an eagle to kill rattlesnakes and bring them back to her like a setter retrieving quail. Then Quince had heard enough. He told Snipes that he'd listened to some haystack-high bullshit in his life but none taller than this eagle yarn. When the other crew members attested it was true, Quince had laughed at the lot of them and said they'd better find some other new hire for their tomfoolery.

But now as he stared at the office porch, Quince had the uneasy feeling that he had come to a place where all manner of strange occurrences were possible, and none of them good.

Henryson turned to Snipes.

"That deadline's Friday, ain't it?"

"Supposed to be."

With the last of the west ridge almost cut, Henryson looked across the valley floor, where four hundred acres of timber remained. At the lowest elevation a few sycamore and sweetgum before they ceded to tulip poplar and hickory, white ash and maple, red oak and beech, one blighted chestnut yet standing. Nearer the crest, green-needled firs and spruce steepled skyward. The steel cables that would carry logs across the valley floor had been braced, but the skidder and McGiffert loader were still dormant, the flatcars empty. The loggers already there could hardly be seen, but their axes caught the morning sun, sent out silver sparks.

"Look at that ridge," Henryson said. "It's slantways as a church roof."

"Meeks said it's best to save the worst for last," Quince opined.

"He's wrong," Henryson said. "You think the snakes is plaguesome now, just wait. They always favor a ridge facing east."

"And we've been herding them that way nine months," Snipes said. "You'd need a flock of eagles to thin them out."

"Ain't no way in hell we'll make that deadline," Henry-son said.

The crew studied the uncut acreage.

"They might try to speed us up like in the cotton mill," Quince said. "My uncle Nebuchadnezzar worked in one and this 'efficiency expert' come in with a watch and timed Uncle Neb changing them bobbins, like it was a race or something, then said Uncle Neb had to do it that speed all day. Uncle Neb asked that fellow if he seen a power cord coming out of his ass. The fellow said no and Uncle Neb said that's right and he quit right then and there."

"They'd slow down time itself give half a chance," Henryson said.

"Who says that ain't soon coming down the pike?" Snipes said.

Meeks walked out of the mess hall. He was nattily dressed in a white linen suit with matching white wing-tips, the pants secured by purple suspenders Snipes greatly admired. When Meeks saw Serena on the office porch, his leisurely pace quickened to a trot.

"There's a fellow you'd not want to be," Snipes said.

"Meeks can't help it come bad weather," Quince said.

"That won't matter to Mrs. Pemberton," Snipes said.

Quince stepped away from the others and unbuttoned his trousers. As he pissed he stared at the west ridge. In a swamp you could cut down trees and know there were still fish swimming around where the trees had been, and on their stumps you'd see frogs and cooters and birds. But here the pale stumps made the land look poxed, as if infected by some dread disease. One that had killed off all the critters too, because Quince hadn't seen a single rabbit, deer, or bird on the land they'd cut. He thought longingly of his Georgia farm, now beneath the surface of a lake. He buttoned up his trousers and rejoined the others.

"We're going to need all the brightness we can find," Snipes said, turning to Quince. "That goes for you especially."

"That trick the eagle done don't mean all of what you've made a claiming for is true," Quince said with forced bravado. "Twenty years I've logged and nary once heard wearing gaudy colors protects a man."

"Cutting timber ain't the same up here," Snipes said. "A swamp's so gloamy colors don't show out."

"That lake has made it even gloamier," Quince said resignedly. "It weren't enough to run us live folks off. Wouldn't even leave our dead folks be. Dug them up like turnips and hauled them off."

"Our folks got run out for that park," Henryson said, turning to meet his cousin's eyes, "but at least they've let our loved ones rest in peace."

"How can we know they truly rest in peace?" Ross replied tersely, then retrieved his ax. He walked uphill to the beech tree he was notching.

"He's got more moody in him than a mule," Quince said softly.

"You lose a wife and children you'd be too," Henryson said quietly, "especially if you think you could have saved them."

"I didn't know that last part," Quince said.

"You know now," Henryson said.

Ross's ax blade struck the beech tree's trunk. The sound ricocheted off the opposite ridge and returned to its source.

Quince went back to limbing as Henryson and Snipes took
up the handles of their crosscut saw. After a glance upward
at a tulip poplar twenty times their height, the two men
began and soon achieved a rhythm, the saw's steady rasps
punctuated by Ross's ax strikes, Quince's blows a softer per-
cussion. A few minutes later Snipes paused and placed a
steel wedge in the trunk. As he reached behind him for
the sledgehammer, Snipes's fingers touched something cold
and coiled. He jerked his hand away just as the copperhead
struck. As it coiled to bite again, Quince's ax severed the
snake's head, but even then its mouth, fangs protracted,
snapped open and shut. Snipes sat down on a stump. The
fang marks looked more like scratches than punctures. As
the rest of the crew gathered around him, Snipes pressed a
finger next to where the snake had struck.

"It's not tender or swelling," Snipes said.

"A dry bite then?" Ross asked, studying the hand and
forearm for red streaks.

"I don't feel no poison," Snipes said, making a fist and
then unclenching it.

"Don't get up yet," Henryson cautioned, placing a hand
on Snipes's shoulder.

After another minute they were certain.

"You sure got lucky, Snipes," Quince said.

Snipes rubbed the sleeve of his red shirt as another
man might rub a rabbit's foot.

"Not a bit of luck," he said. "It was the brightness."

Snipes picked up the sledgehammer and drove the
wedge deeper into the tree.

The saw's teeth raked across the trunk seven more

times before the tulip poplar began to tremble. Snipes and Henryson pulled out the saw and yelled "timber." The tree creaked and tottered, then paused as if the ridge that held it upright for over a century might yet anchor it. A last loud crackling and the tulip poplar crashed earthward.

# 2

The road, barely wider than the car itself, tilted and swerved down the mountain as if designed with drunken malevolence. There was no guardrail, only a long falling toward death that Galloway, their one-handed driver, appeared oblivious to as he again let go of the steering wheel to raise a cigarette to his lips. Calhoun, who shared the back seat with Brandonkamp, appeared unalarmed, perhaps because he'd emptied a whiskey flask on the train ride from Asheville to Sylva. From what Brandonkamp had heard about Serena Pemberton, she might have commanded the driver to unnerve him deliberately, gain an early advantage before he made the agreed-upon inspection of the equipment.

Then the road straightened, and for the first time he saw the valley. From this vantage, the glistening railroad tracks, the engine and its flatcars, resembled what a child might discover under a Christmas tree. Soon he could see the camp, smoke rising above the mess hall, beside it a weathered two-storey farmhouse and a smaller A-frame building that served as the office. Behind these buildings were two makeshift bunkhouses where the loggers slept. The valley floor was, except for a pasture, a welter of stumps and slash and mud, the ridges the same except for a portion of the east-facing flank. The unlogged portion appeared formidable, steep-graded and thick-timbered.

The Pierce-Arrow made a last long plunge. The engine whined and both passengers held on to the side doors as their bodies tilted forward. The land leveled and they entered the camp, passing the mess hall and farmhouse and stopping in front of the office, where two dark-suited Pinkertons smoked cigars. Brandonkamp and Calhoun got out of the car.

"In yonder," Galloway said, waving his hand toward the A-frame.

Unlike at the train station, Brandonkamp could see Galloway more clearly—the sinister stitch-scarred wrist evoking past violence, the conspicuously worn dagger auguring a desire for more. But the man's eyes were even more disconcerting. *As soon kill you as look at you,* Brandonkamp had heard men described, chimerically it now seemed, because this man appeared to be truly weighing the option, and favoring the first.

"I want to have a look at the machinery," Brandonkamp said as Galloway drove off to park the car.

"I assure you it's in the condition she told you," Calhoun said. "Whatever else one can say of her, she is a woman who always honors her contracts."

"I prefer to check anyway," Brandonkamp said.

Calhoun had other business with Mrs. Pemberton, so he went on inside. Brandonkamp set his briefcase on the porch and walked over to inspect the skidder and McGiffert loader, listened for any dissonance between the gears and levers. Then he had the operator pause and climbed onto the skidder himself to examine it further. Brandonkamp inspected the loader in a similar manner. The condition of lesser equipment told much about the care of the expensive items, so he went to the east ridge and joined the loggers, found their axes and crosscut saws well maintained. He calculated the amount of timber and the time required to cut it. Mud clung to his alligator shoes and pants cuffs, but a small price for confirmation that, as he'd expected after such a hard winter and rainy spring, the deadline wouldn't be met. Only then did he head toward the office. As he crossed the yard, he noticed an old woman sitting in a wooden chair. She was dressed all in black, her face bonneted. He tipped his fedora but the woman didn't acknowledge him.

The Pinkertons were gone when Brandonkamp stepped onto the office porch. He picked up his briefcase and entered the front room. Serena Pemberton and Calhoun studied a map so large that it draped over the desk like a tablecloth. She wore dust-colored jodhpurs and a green poplin shirt and was taller than he'd expected. Her high cheekbones, narrow nose, and slender lips were striking, but most of all the eyes—gray but gold-flecked, more oval than round. Her body similar, distinctly feminine but thin, though thin wasn't exactly right. *Honed* seemed a better word. No rings gilded her long fingers, the nails cut to the quick. Her only seeming excess was her shoulder-length blond hair.

He had expected her to be different, less attractive, less feminine. He could see why George Pemberton had been smitten. Impressive, but still a woman, and now without the husband who'd made Pemberton Lumber Company so successful. Brandonkamp moved forward and extended his hand. Her palm was more callused than his, her grip firm.

"First of all, my condolences," Brandonkamp said. "I met your husband once on a visit to Boston. An exceptional man."

"He tried hard to be so," Serena said.

Brandonkamp looked at the map and Calhoun pointed to a red circle.

"Ten square miles of prime mahogany," Calhoun said.

"Very impressive," Brandonkamp agreed. "It seems you've found Brazil much to your liking."

"I have," Serena said.

"And dealing with a foreign government?"

"I find their candor refreshing."

"How so, if I may presume to ask?"

"They don't pretend that they can't be bought," Serena said.

Brandonkamp turned to Calhoun.

"Once the camp is fully operating, will you be going to Brazil as well?"

Calhoun shook his head, a sardonic smile on his face.

"As regards Mrs. Pemberton and her ventures, it behooves a partner to leave all decisions to her alone."

Serena rolled up the map and placed it inside a tin cylinder. Calhoun sat down in one of the room's three ladder-back chairs. Brandonkamp sat also, but Serena remained standing. *Never underestimate this woman*, Calhoun had warned, and Brandonkamp had not as he and Mrs. Pemberton discussed the sale of the logging equipment via telegram. But she may have underestimated him.

"You've found the equipment to your satisfaction?"

"Very well maintained," Brandonkamp answered, "but as far as the July thirty-first deadline, I must remind you that there is a ten-percent price deduction if it's not met, and that includes having all equipment loaded on the train."

"Having the equipment loaded was not discussed," Serena said. "That is your responsibility."

Brandonkamp wasn't sure how he expected her to react, but except for her eyes locking on his, there was no change in her face. He withdrew a thick document from his brief-case. He turned to a back page and set it on the desk.

"A sentence was added to the final contract. As you can see, your man Meeks signed in your absence. There were a number of pages, so perhaps he missed the addition. Or simply forgot to tell you."

Calhoun's eyes briefly met Brandonkamp's, conveying little. For a few moments the room was silent. Behind Brandonkamp a match was struck. He turned and saw Galloway leaning against a doorjamb. He hadn't heard the man enter. The highlander raised a cigarette to his mouth and flicked the match out the door. He inhaled and let the smoke drift toward Brandonkamp.

Brandonkamp set the soles of his shoes firmly on the floor, as if the planks had become very slippery. They were trying to unnerve him enough to drop the proviso, but he also knew that if he did give in to this woman, a gadabout like Calhoun would have it known all over the region. He could almost hear the laughter as Calhoun told how the newcomer had been intimidated into backing down.

"With the amount of acreage left to cut," Brandonkamp said in a conciliatory tone, "the matter of loading the equipment will be moot. I'm afraid it looks as if that ten-percent reduction is assured."

"To catch the next train, you need to leave now," Serena said, and turned to Galloway. "Have one of the men saddle my horse. When you get back, I'll be on the ridge with the crews."

As he and Calhoun waited for Galloway to bring around the Pierce-Arrow, Brandonkamp gazed at the east ridge and felt a surge of confidence. Come Friday at midnight sharp, he'd be here, and with him Calhoun to witness the lapsed deadline. As the Pierce-Arrow pulled up in front of the office porch, Brandonkamp told himself that if he could just survive the drive back to the station, everything would be fine.

*The mountain lion was the first to depart the valley. The front paw lost years back to a trap's steel teeth was warning enough. As the trees began to fall, others followed: black bear and bobcat, otter and mink, some in pairs, some singly. Then beaver and weasel, deer and muskrat, groundhog and fox. After them raccoon and rabbit, opossum and chipmunk, squirrel and vole, deer mouse and shrew . . .*

# 3

When the bell rang three times, signaling it was noon, the crew set down their tools and ate. Two water boys made their midday trek across the ridge, wooden barrels strapped to the mules they rode. Some men refilled jars or canteens while others used the tin dipper to drink from the barrel. When Snipes finished his lunch, he settled his back against a stump and took out the newspaper Noah Holt, both train engineer and postmaster, bought in Sylva for him. Snipes perused the front page, then lit his briar pipe and flapped the paper open. Tobacco fumes rose from behind the paper like smoke signals.

"So what's your fishwrapper got to say today?" Henryson asked Snipes.

Snipes lowered his newspaper just enough to peer over it.

"More banks is closed," Snipes said. "Poor folks is getting poorer."

"There ain't nary a bit of news in that," Henryson said.

"Capone is headed to the hoosegow now," Snipes said. "Seems you can murder all the folks you want as long as you don't cheat the government."

"The missus must keep all her taxes paid," Henryson said.

"She's always been a conscientious woman," Snipes acknowledged, "even pays them Raleigh politicians some extra just in case she needs a favor."

Ross stood and gazed down into the valley. Meeks, suitcase in hand, came out of the farmhouse where he'd lived since November. He walked toward the bunkhouses, head down like a chastened schoolchild as Serena, on horseback, and Galloway, on foot, moved slowly below the ridge to observe each crew's progress. Henryson came and stood beside his cousin.

"What are you looking at so steely-eyed?" Henryson asked, then saw the small, black-clothed figure at the valley's center. She was seated in a high-backed mahogany armchair. There, amid the vast floor of stumps and slash, Galloway's mother appeared almost regal. Snipes and Quince joined them.

"Come out to see her boy off to work," Henryson quipped. "She's ever the doting mother, don't you think?"

"Probably hoping the sun will warm her up," Snipes said, "as is the way of many other a reptile."

"That hag is pointed west toward Tennessee," Ross said. "They're going after that Harmon girl again."

"Well nigh a miracle she dodged them once," Snipes said. "No one else has, unless it's Joel Vaughn. They never found his body. But the others . . ."

The men became somber.

"What Galloway and his knife done to McDowell, to do that to a man before he killed him," Henryson said, then paused. For a few moments, the men looked elsewhere instead of at one another. "I'm hoping they won't have the time to find her," Henryson finally said. "They'll only be here till this valley's logged."

"They'll make the time," Ross said.

The two beefy young men came out of the mess hall. They were still in suits but wore badges now.

"Them is Pinkertons," Snipes said.

"Pinkertons?" Quince said worriedly. "There ain't no talk of striking in this camp."

"They might be wanting to snuff it before it starts," Snipes said. "Them fellows up north has lit the powder keg." Snipes turned the pages as if fanning himself, found what he looked for and held it outward. *Twelve Injured in Union Riot.*

"Maybe it's time for us to do the same," Ross said. "An injury to one's an injury to all."

"That's Wobbly talk and best you don't repeat it," Quince warned, "especially with Pinkertons around."

The men went back to work. Because the east ridge was so steep, balance was less certain. Henryson and Snipes made divots to secure their footing. Quince did the same. Ross took no such precautions, nor did he notice a rattlesnake until he almost stepped on it. The snake struck his boot, then glided smoothly down the ridge, head aloft as the satin-black body skimmed the ground.

Shortly thereafter Quince yelled "sarpent" and cleaved a black-and-white snake into four pieces.

"That's a chain snake, you durn onion head," Henryson said. "It eats them other ones that got the poison."

"How's I to know?" Quince replied sulkily. "Open its mouth and see if it has fangs?"

At three o'clock, the water boys made their rounds again. By this time Serena and Galloway had worked their way halfway across the ridge, Serena giving instructions to each crew, occasionally dismounting to scrutinize work or instruct how to do a task better. As they approached Snipes's crew, every man except Ross stopped working and bared his head. Ross continued notching a white oak as Serena got off the horse.

"You need Mullins to sharpen the teeth on that saw," she told Snipes, and walked over to the felled poplar Quince was limbing.

"Can't you see you're not trimming those branches close enough?" Serena said, taking Quince's ax and swinging. When she stepped back, the branch was sheared so cleanly it might have been sanded.

"I promise that I'll do it better, ma'am," Quince said as Galloway stepped alongside Ross.

"The blade of a broad ax don't work good for notching," Galloway said. "Move out of the way so the missus can see it."

Ross swung again, the blade passing inches from Galloway's right leg. Chips flew. Ross freed the ax head and met Galloway's glare.

"Time to go check the upper ridge," Serena said. "His notching is fine."

"Best remember you some manners, Ross," Galloway said, "else you'll learn them again the hard way."

Galloway's index finger brushed the dagger looped around his neck. He did it with no more concern than a man flicking off a piece of lint. Still looking at Ross, Galloway raised the finger, now streaked with blood.

"That's not a man you want to trifle with," Snipes said once Galloway and Serena were out of sight. "A man like you who knows his math can cipher the percentages ain't good."

"Yeah, I know all about percentages," Ross said.

The men went back to work. An hour later a nearby logger slipped and almost cut his foot off. Snipes's crew watched as the man hobbled across the valley floor toward the blue boxcar that served as office and infirmary for Watson, no doctor but a stretcher-bearer in the Great War. Only a few yards from the boxcar was the camp's graveyard, their proximity noted by the crews with varying degrees of irony and dismay. Eight crosses rose inside the split-rail fence.

"I suspect that boneyard's going to crowd up quick," Snipes said, and no one argued otherwise.

As the afternoon wore on, the last sycamore and silver birch fell. Stands of tulip, poplar, and hickory appeared, which, along with the increasing slant of the land, made the work more arduous. At six o'clock Snipes's crew joined the other men shogging down the ridge.

"Appears the law is making a social call," Henryson said, gesturing at a black Ford with SHERIFF'S PATROL on the side.

On the mess hall porch, flanked to the left by Serena and Meeks, stood a purfled young man dressed in a brown Cheviot suit, a silver star on the coat's lapel. His black hair glistened with pomade. The Pinkertons stood to his right, arms crossed. Galloway joined them, accompanied by a crew foreman named Murrell. The loggers gathered in front of the porch and grew silent.

Serena motioned to Meeks and he stepped forward. Neck tucked, narrow shoulders hunched, he resembled a cautious turtle. Meeks looked at the loggers he'd commanded for nine months. What he saw in their faces did not hearten him.

"From now on Mrs. Pemberton is in charge," he said, then joined the men he'd just addressed.

Serena Pemberton approached the railing. On level ground she was taller than most of the loggers, but she towered over them from the porch. Many of the men had worked at the Cataloochee camp and, as then, they viewed their employer with a mixture of awe and trepidation. Her eyes passed over the veterans to settle, one at a time, on the recent hires. None seemed to impress her. Her gaze widened again.

"You knew my deadline last year when you came here to work," Serena said. "You've been well fed and housed. You took every paycheck knowing the deadline. We *will* finish on time, and because of Meeks's further incompetence, that includes having all equipment loaded on the train. Any man who quits or lags gets no paycheck for this month."

Incredulous looks appeared on many of the men's faces. Murmurs of discontent were heard.

"If you've got something to say, say it out loud," Serena said.

A foreman named Bolger timidly raised his hand.

"Ma'am, my crew won't ease up until nary a tree's on that ridge, but there's not time enough to make that deadline."

"We'll make the time," Serena answered.

Bolger looked at the east ridge.

"Ma'am, I'm just saying what I believe."

"Get your belongings out of the bunkhouse, and make sure you leave your ax," Serena said.

"Ma'am," Bolger stammered.

Galloway said something to the Pinkertons, who nodded and stepped off the porch, but Bolger was already leaving.

"Anyone else who believes the same, go now," Serena said. "We'll be bringing in more men to help." She turned to Zack Murrell. "I've promoted Murrell so he'll be responsible for conveying most orders. If you've got a problem, go to him."

"Too bad you didn't get the promotion," Henryson said quietly to Snipes. "From the look of it, Murrell's wishing the same."

"Anything else?" Serena asked the men below her. No hand rose. "If not, Sheriff Bowden has something to say."

The young man gave a nervous nod to Serena and stepped forward. He held a piece of paper, studying it a few moments before addressing his audience.

"I've come to ask your help in an investigation about the death of my predecessor, Sheriff McDowell. We need to locate Rachel Harmon, whom many of you should remember, since she worked in the kitchen at the Cataloochee camp." Bowden looked at the paper again and nodded at the Pinkertons. "We will be assisted by professionals, but we also need your help. Any names of out-of-state relatives or friends she may be staying with, or even places she might have mentioned, could be important. There's a fifty-dollar reward for anyone who helps us find her and the child."

As Bowden went to stand beside Serena, Galloway stepped beside the mess hall's doorway, in his hand a black-and-white photograph of Rachel Harmon and her son.

"In case you forgot, here's the look of her."

Galloway held the photograph toward the loggers a few moments, then placed it against the wall, held it there with his forearm while he pulled a spring-back knife from his pocket. The blade locked into place and Galloway jabbed its point through the photograph and into the wood, burying the tip in Rachel Harmon's throat.

"There's one other thing," Serena said, nodding at Galloway, who left the porch to stand among the loggers.

"Your watches," Galloway said, holding out his felt hat.

Most of the men possessing timepieces were crew foremen, all of whom knew Galloway from the previous camp. They did not ask when or if the watches would be returned but silently dug into their pockets or tugged on brass and silver fobs. They set them in their palms and came forth singly to drop their watches into Galloway's hat.

When the last timepiece was surrendered, the Pinkertons barring the mess hall's entrance stepped aside.

"Can you make out the heads or tails of this?" Henryson asked Snipes.

"I've got a notion," Snipes answered. "Let's just see what tomorrow's weather is like."

# 4

Ever prudent, even as a child, his mother had said of Meeks. So she'd accepted the necessity of his leaving Boston for the wilds of Carolina, where he'd be Pemberton Lumber Company's head bookkeeper. To be employed by such a prominent family was a rare opportunity. True, the scandalous hussy George Pemberton married gave one pause, but Meeks would be working for George, not his wife, and since the Carolina venture was nearly finished, the Pembertons and Meeks would soon return to Boston. At most nine months, he'd assured his mother.

Now, as he snapped the suitcase's brass locks shut, Meeks knew he'd not been prudent enough. Just weeks after hiring him, George Pemberton had died, but Meeks stayed on when Mrs. Pemberton offered the promotion. She would be in Brazil, a continent away, leaving Meeks in charge of the whole North Carolina operation. All he had to do was make the deadline he'd been given. Before agreeing, he'd researched company records and found, based on past performance, that the date looked easily doable, so much so that he promised Serena Pemberton it would be met. But the snow had been heavier than in a decade. How was that his fault? And having to run the camp *and* be the book-keeper, how could he be expected to notice a one-sentence proviso in a twenty-page contract? She had humiliated him in front of the whole camp. Then as if that were not enough, sent him to this bunkhouse to sleep among a bunch of snoring ruffians.

No, he wouldn't put up with it. He slipped on his white linen jacket. Besides, though he'd never actually believed the stories about Serena Pemberton murdering those who fell out of favor, the prudent move was to leave, and to do so discreetly. Why tempt fate, especially when Mrs. Pemberton would be aware, as was most of America, of Fred Ries, the bookkeeper who'd recently helped bring about Capone's downfall.

Meeks stepped out of the bunkhouse, took matches from his shirt pocket, and lit the lantern. Soon he came to his former office. The Pierce-Arrow was parked there, which could get him to the depot in ten minutes if Galloway hadn't demanded the keys. They'd taken his strap watch too, yet another humiliation, but it couldn't be much past ten o'clock. At midnight a train would take him to Asheville, from there eventually to Boston. The walk was only two miles. He had plenty of time.

Soon a full moon rose, but not a single star emerged. No doubt the highlanders would find some portent in such a thing. An owl seen in daylight, a broken mirror, a design in a spider's web—all were signs of something to these people, and that something was almost always bad. Just hours ago as Meeks announced he was no longer in charge, they'd stared up at him as if the porch were a scaffold.

Enough of such thoughts, Meeks told himself. Once he was on the train, all would be fine. In less than a week Serena Pemberton would be back in Brazil and Meeks would give her no cause to return. He'd keep his mouth closed about the political donations and tax evasions. After all, safe on another continent, she'd realize Meeks would be indicting only himself.

He quickened his pace but soon had to stop to catch his breath and rest his arms. He hadn't thought it would be this hard. In the Pierce-Arrow two miles had not felt far at all, and uphill had only been a matter of shifting gears. Meeks was sweating. Dust coated his shoes and pants cuffs. The road made a sharp ascent and he was quickly breathing hard again. The lantern and suitcase felt like iron weights some circus strongman might lift. As if that weren't enough, the wingtips blistered his heels, each step a fresh scald of pain. *Get on your feet, happy days are here again.* Where had he last heard that song? Not here in this godforsaken place, he knew. The only music in this valley was the highlanders' doleful ballads.

The road straightened and Meeks saw before him yet another long ascent. He suddenly felt unable to muster another step. For the first time, he feared he'd perhaps made a mistake leaving the camp at night and in secret. How could Mrs. Pemberton not suspect treachery for his doing so? Even if she hadn't thought to harm him before, now she would have real cause. Once on the train he'd be safe, but what if he didn't get to the depot on time? The next train to Asheville wouldn't arrive until eight a.m. By then she'd know he'd left. She'd send her ogre to find him, and the first place he'd look would be the depot. Meeks's head felt like a hive, thoughts darting in and out, no one he could hold and be sure of.

But that was not true. There was *one:* he had to get to the depot before twelve. Meeks looked up at the midsummer night. Still no stars, but the moon's light would surely be enough. There was no shoulder here, only a sheer of granite on one side, a long fall on the other. He pitched the lantern into the dark as he would a horseshoe. The glass globe shattered louder than he'd wished, but this far from camp it didn't matter.

Then Meeks thought he heard his name called, though from where he could not say. He didn't hear it again. *Just my imagination,* he told himself. Carrying only the suitcase now, he resumed walking. The moon was higher, its light spilling across the road. At the top of the rise, the road leveled. To his right the ground conjoined with the valley's north ridge, where, last November, the logging had begun. Just nine months ago his future had been all bright promise. Once the valley was logged, Serena Pemberton would send him back to Boston, where, as head of Pemberton Lumber's U.S. operations, he'd be feted as a rising captain of industry. That had been the dream, not this nightmare.

Meeks stopped again and set the suitcase down. He looked up the road and still saw no town lights, but he had to be close. Once around the next curve, Meeks assured himself, he would see the lights of the town, of the depot, then the train with window after window, each a warm square of light.

A childhood memory came of an evening only days before Christmas, bright packages already beneath the tree.

He'd been tucked in bed by his mother, the light turned off, but he'd gotten up to look out the bay window. Snow flurries swirled around a streetlight, the cobblestones shiny from their moisture. No vehicles, no one walking. How cold and lonely the streetlight had looked, but he was inside warm and with his family. As he heard their voices downstairs, tears had gathered in the corners of his eyes. *Two days and you'll be back in Boston,* Meeks told himself, and picked up the suitcase.

Then Meeks did see a light, not ahead but behind him. It was Galloway, a lantern swaying before him. He trotted ahead of Mrs. Pemberton, she astride the horse whose pale coat appeared to cast its own light. Meeks stumbled off the right slope and fell to the ground. He didn't think they'd seen him. He opened the suitcase, pushed aside clothing and toiletries, and withdrew an oval-glassed daguerreotype of his mother, a Waterman fountain pen, and a clean pair of socks, stuffed it all into his pants pockets.

Keeping low, he moved into a wasteland leveled by ax and saw. Last November, he'd smoked a Partagas cigar as the tract's last tree fell, but the same denuded landscape he'd celebrated was now exacting its revenge. The land shadowless, moonlight fell full upon his hunched form. Yet bright as the moon shown, the stumps and slash blended with the ground. Every few steps he fell, got up, and fell again.

He'd progressed half a furlong when the lantern's light appeared where he'd left the road. The light began moving toward him. Meeks could see the north ridge's crest, which marked the end of Pemberton Lumber Company's property. If he could get over it, there were trees to conceal him.

Meeks hobbled up to the crest, only then looked back. Below, the whole valley could be seen, thousands upon thousands of stumps. In the moonlight, they looked like gravestones. Only the uncut portion of the east ridge denied the illusion. Nothing in the valley or ridges moved, except the light that stalked him. Meeks went down the opposite flank, much of the moonlight hidden by the canopy. He descended low to the ground and, feet first, sliding at times before being braked by a tree. When he looked back, Meeks saw only darkness.

Then the woods opened and Meeks heard water rubbing against a bank. He stepped closer. Upstream, only a silky darkness, but downstream the river widened. The moon fell upon it there, rocks glinting midriver, so perhaps shoals. Not far beyond that, where the river narrowed again, something else. He thought it a dam, then realized it was a covered bridge and knew where he was. Meeks started downstream, struggled through a tangle of mountain laurel, but after that a wide bare bank. He heard the hoot of a train. It couldn't be midnight yet, but an earlier train did go to Chattanooga. Anywhere out of this hellscape would be fine. He touched his back pocket, felt the wallet still there. Torn and frayed as he was, he'd likely be mistaken for a hobo, but even a hobo's money bought a ticket.

He stepped onto a road latticed by wagon wheels. Across the river, Meeks saw the depot's lights. As he approached the bridge's dark mouth, he decided Chattanooga might be better. They would expect him to head to Asheville. Meeks looked upriver. Only darkness. The train slowed to a stop in front of the depot. Brakes hissed. A bell clanged. He was going to make it.

Meeks stepped inside the bridge, felt the planks under his battered feet. There was no light, so he put a hand on the wall to guide him. Meeks took a tentative step, then a second, and the darkness deepened. He remembered the matchbox and patted his shirt. It wasn't there. Then a match rasped, summoned forth a flicker of flame. A wick caught and, as if rising out of the lantern itself, Galloway's face appeared.

Meeks took two slow backward steps. As he turned to run, Mrs. Pemberton came out of the woods. He leaped off the bank and landed amid the boulder-strewn shallows. He stumbled forward and dove underwater. Breaking the surface, Meeks found himself neck-deep in the river. He turned and saw Serena on horseback in the shallows, her left hand circling as if beckoning him to return. Then something floated toward him in the air. Directly overhead, the lariat stalled, dropped into the water. For a moment it lay flaccid. Then the rope snapped taut around his neck. Meeks tried to free the noose, legs kicking to keep from going under. Serena secured the rope to the pommel. She turned the horse and Meeks was jerked forward, dragged headfirst toward shore where he saw Galloway, knife at the ready. The water shallowed and Meeks's right shoulder slammed against a boulder. As it did, the rope jerked his head sideways and the neck bone snapped.

Meeks's eyes were still open, but they did not see Galloway cut free the noose, unclasp the suspenders from the linen pants. Nor did Meeks see the henchman's one hand wield a hickory branch like a peavey stick, prod his body out of the shallows into the river's main current, and, as Meeks drifted downstream, his eyes, though looking upward, did not see the morning sun when its angled beams gilded the river. He did not see in that same sky the first dark forms assembling, then slowly kettling downward, somber-suited ferrymen, who asked of him no coin as they accompanied him on his passage.

*As silt choked the creek, the speckled trout left first,*
*and then the greenfin darter and warpaint shiner, blacktail*
*redhorse and rosyside dace, and after them the longnose*
*darter and mottled sculpin, creek chub and river chub, and*
*after that the snapping turtle and painted turtle, bullfrog and*
*pickerel frog, the mudpuppy and red-spotted newt . . .*

## 5

After he and Serena returned, Galloway went to his room, hoping for a last bit of sleep. His mother, who'd waked him earlier to announce Meeks had fled, lay in the bed beside his. He didn't tell her they had found Meeks and killed him. She already knew, just as she knew they'd find Meeks by a bridge. *You'll find him where a man can walk across water,* she'd said.

Only once, when he was seven years old, had Galloway tried to lie to her. For two nights he'd seen bright-colored lights in a field across the railroad tracks. He had no notion of what was in the field, but a man in town had winked at another man and said wonders aplenty were there. So he'd asked his mother for a nickel to buy licorice whips at Darby's Store, but instead had crossed the railroad tracks to join others wandering the sawdust-strewn fairground. Paintings on each tent did indeed promise wonders: a snake long as a telegraph pole, a woman with a beard, a man eating fire and another a live chicken. Outside the tents, there were also things to eat. Candy apples, taffy, popcorn, and ice cream. His eyes and belly were fighting for the nickel, until he came to the last tent.

Galloway stared at the painting draped to the right of the entrance: a pretty woman with long black hair that curled snaky to her shoulders, her privates top and bottom barely covered. But that was not what held his eye. Swords floated in the air, each aimed at the woman who spread a hand before her as if trying to hide behind it, her mouth open in a silent scream. He counted the swords 1 2 3 4 5 6.

A man stood at the entrance selling tickets. He wore a red-and-white striped coat and white pants and had a wooden cane in his hand. *Come inside if you dare,* the man said, *and watch a brave woman face certain death. Only ten cents, ladies and gents.* He'd rubbed the nickel between his thumb and finger. It was hard but greasy too, and he could feel the *V* etched on the coin and it was pointing at the tent, like even the nickel was saying this was what he had to see. He felt his flesh stir. *Looks like you taken a shine to her, boy,* the man said, pointing the cane at the front of Galloway's britches. *But yours ain't the first pecker she's raised. Likely she'll raise quite a few more before we leave this town, but it'll cost more than a nickel.*

The man laughed and looked past him, resumed calling passersby. Laughing at me, he knew, but he still wasn't going to leave.

*I'll give you this here nickel if you let me in,* he told the man.

He said it twice before the man looked down at him.

*It ain't for children,* the man said, and called out that the show was about to begin. But no one else came forward. The man gave a quick look around.

*Give me it.*

Inside was a small wooden stage, on it an upturned

metal box the size and shape of a steamer trunk. The box
had a door and soon the woman came on the stage, gave a
bow, and got inside. There wasn't room enough to stand so
she scrunched up as best she could. A man with a mustache
closed the door and bolted it so the woman couldn't get out.
There were three slits on the door and three in the back and
three on each of the sides. So she can fetch her breath, Galloway had figured. Men sat on benches around the stage,
but he stood so he could see better. Another man came on
the stage, holding six swords in his arms. The mustached
man took one and walked over to the metal box. He put its
tip in the door's highest slit and pushed the sword in until
the tip came out the other side. The man didn't take out
the sword, but instead went to the side and sent the second
sword through its top slit.

*Ducked them both*, he told himself, then figured the
woman ducked even lower when the mustached man sent
swords through the middle. But with the four sword tips
poking through the box, he knew she was cornered good.
The man went back to the door and slid the fifth sword
into the lowest slit. The blade stopped halfway. The tent
was silent as the man put both hands on the handle and
shoved it on through, then had to push even harder before
the sixth sword's tip poked out. *He done went and murdered
her dead*, a man on the front row shouted and ran out of
the tent. The mustached man slowly withdrew each sword,
then stood a few moments in front of the big box looking
real sad. *He ain't gonna let us see her*, he thought, and that
ain't a bit fair. But the man turned and slowly unbolted
the door. Galloway moved closer, hands gripping the stage
as he stood on his tiptoes. The door swung open and the

woman came out and raised her arms with not a drop of blood on her.

He ran outside and yanked at the man's coat until the man whirled around.

*She didn't get kilt. I want my nickel back.*

He didn't leave until the man raised his cane and swatted him. As he re-crossed the railroad tracks, he saw a penny placed on a rail. It made the penny lucky to get squashed by a train. He looked around, saw no one, and figured the penny would bring more luck for him if it wasn't squashed. He went to Darby's Store, bought a single licorice whip and went home, chomping it to get his teeth black and sticky, still chewing when he entered the room where his mother sat facing the fireplace just as he'd left her. She stopped rocking just long enough to tell him something he could not fully understand then: *It won't be the last time you get disappointed like that.*

And it wasn't. Because last October, three decades after entering the fairground tent, the adult Galloway saw another woman trapped inside a metal box, though this metal box was rolling on wheels and Rachel Harmon wasn't even a full-grown woman, just a girl and her bastard child. That time, though, Galloway was the one who'd held the blade and barred the way out. Had her and her brat dead to rights, but the bitch had clubbed him with something. Then he was lying beside the tracks, watching the train's red caboose fade into the night, carrying Rachel Harmon and the child away.

Galloway shifted to face his sleeping mother, or he guessed she slept. He couldn't even know if she was in the here and now. For her, time was a road traveled in both directions. Over the years she'd told him many things that would happen, including how a woman would save his life and he'd be bound to that woman ever after because the two of them could never die unless they died together. He'd asked when that would be, and his mother answered she'd never wanted to know that any more than when she herself would die. But she had warned him and Serena Pemberton, the woman he was bound to, that the Harmon girl and her child could pose a danger if allowed to live.

For nine months he'd been patient. Though she'd tried, in Brazil his mother couldn't conjure where the girl was. Not being on the same continent, the sea—something had interfered. Galloway had worried she might have lost sight of the girl and child forever. But once they'd arrived in Florida, his mother had felt a faint awareness.

Galloway touched the lanyard, then the dagger itself, and closed his eyes. As it did most nights, the ache began. He rubbed the stumped forearm, though where the hand itself had been was the ache's source. Last summer when the ax severed the hand, his mother had him bury it with the palm facing up. That way it'll know which way to dig, she'd told him. He did so, burying the hand on a sandy creek bank. When the aching began, Galloway sensed that the hand had begun to stir.

Rubbing the stump didn't ease the ache, so Galloway did what he always did to ease himself asleep. He thought about the hand digging out of the sand, watched it in his mind like it was a picture show. First a couple of black fingernails, then the fingers, and last the full hand. As he grew drowsy, Galloway watched the hand flip over and crawl up the bank, head over the mountains into Tennessee to pick up the trail. When it got to a creek or river, the fingertips touched the surface and crossed over like a water strider. There'd be hungry foxes and raccoons and maybe even a panther, but the index and middle fingers would rear up like fangs and the animals would back off same as they would a tarantula. Maybe the land would level out or maybe it wouldn't, but the hand would know exactly where to go. It'd trail the girl and her bastard down railroad tracks and city streets and dirt roads and never lose the scent.

Galloway was dreaming now as the hand finally found its prey, not inside a metal box but in a dark room. The Harmon girl was asleep, the child beside her. The hand crawled through an open window and then over the floor and up a bedpost. It killed the girl first. Then scuttled across the covers and latched on to the child's throat, and in that instant hand and wrist were one flesh and he was whole again.

The throbbing woke Galloway and he rubbed the wrist. *Soon,* he assured himself. *Soon.*

# 6

When Rachel first arrived in Seattle, she had gazed out of a bus window at the ocean. It had frightened her to find nothing but emptiness as far as she could see. Even the sky had the sun and clouds, at night the moon and stars. She had walked around Seattle for months but avoided streets with an ocean view. *To never see the end of something.* That was what Rachel had feared since barely escaping Galloway's knife. Knoxville to Omaha, Denver to San Francisco, Portland to Seattle, on that trip across the country she was always looking behind her, at each station checking the platform before coming or going, searching shadows for a cigarette's glow. During those first days in Seattle, it had been worse. Each time she'd turned a street corner or opened a door, Rachel knew Galloway could be waiting, knife in hand. She rented an upstairs room at Miss Hill's boardinghouse, hoping with other people around she'd feel safer, but each night she slept with the bowie knife under her pillow.

At first, Seattle had overwhelmed her. Trolleys and automobiles came from all directions and the buildings all crowded together, street after street. Rachel thought she could never get used to being around so many people, the constant bells and whistles and sirens, the smells that burned your nose or made your stomach queasy. Even in the room she rented at Miss Hill's boardinghouse, she heard the traffic on the street, people talking on the sidewalk, other boarders moving about in the hallways. But things gradually got better. She found Frink Park, where there were trees and grass and even a creek she and Jacob could sit beside and listen to. She got work at Mr. and Mrs. Bjorkland's café. They were kind to her, even brought a crib up from their basement so Jacob could stay in the café's kitchen while Rachel worked. *We can make a life here,* she'd whispered to Jacob one night, *and it'll be a good life.*

But even in the midst of this new life, lessons learned in her old one remained, most of all that the world contained more knowledge than might be seen in the light of day. The call of an owl three nights in a row, a bone-pale moon or a falling star, all were portents. Dreams were the same, inklings of not-yet-seen realities or, if heeded, realities possibly avoided. On the night before her father had died, Rachel had dreamed of a woman, her face hidden beneath a black veil, a bloody knife in her hand. Rachel had told her father about the dream the next morning, but it had gone unheeded. Later that same morning, Serena Pemberton would hand Rachel the bloody knife that had killed her father.

Last night she'd dreamed that her and Jacob were looking at the ocean when a wooden ship appeared, far out but coming toward shore. It had only a single sail and that sail was black. A man stood on the wooden bow, a silver cross dangling from the necklace he wore. But as the ship came closer, Rachel saw it was not a cross. Grinning, the man raised his stumped forearm and waved. As the ship entered the harbor, Rachel looked up and down the shore and saw that she and Jacob were alone.

# 7

The next morning the bell awakened them from their dreams. The men dressed quickly and left the bunkhouse, some rubbing their eyes as they moved through the dark toward the mess hall's lights. The shay engine was already parked uptrack of the skidder, so Snipes retrieved his newspaper from Noah Holt before joining his crew. As he entered the mess hall, Snipes saw the wall clock above the kitchen was gone. Servers bustled around the wooden tables and benches with a seldom-seen haste. Coffee mugs were refilled before raised overhead, extra creamers and sugar bowls brought. As quickly as one huge yellowware bowl emptied, another brimming with grits or eggs or sawmill gravy replaced it. Bread baskets and meat platters were whisked away and returned, the biscuits so hot men burned their fingers.

"She's got them stepping lively, that's for sure," Snipes said as a server exchanged another bowl.

Quince yawned.

"It seems a might bit early to be up."

"It is," Henryson said. "If that bell clanged at half past

five, we'd have seen at least a smudge of dawn. But there's no watch or clock to argue it."

"I wonder where Mr. Meeks is at?" Quince asked.

"I'd narrow it to heaven or to hell," Snipes said.

"Dead, you figure," Ross said grimly.

"Look at Galloway and argue not," Snipes said.

At the back table Galloway sat between his mother and Serena. He wore his usual chambray shirt and denim pants, but purple suspenders had replaced his belt.

"Galloway used to give them a good day's start," Henryson said.

"He's making up for lost time, same as us," Snipes said.

"Lord God," Quince said. "What sort of hell pit am I in?"

"Now Galloway's got some bright protecting too," Henryson told Snipes.

"What's looking after him ain't got no brightness," Ross answered, shifting his gaze to Galloway's mother.

Quince also stared at the old woman. The table's bench was bolted to the planked wall, and the tiny woman appeared not so much seated as propped like a doll on a store shelf. Above the thin stalk of neck, inside the black bonnet, receded a face as wrinkled as a walnut. In her mouth no teeth, only deeper darkness. But it was the eyes that Quince was most attentive to. They were cauled with cataracts but he knew those eyes saw plenty. Quince watched longer and realized that what he'd assumed one more tall tale was true. The woman never appeared to blink.

"You best not gander at her very long," Henryson warned Quince.

Quince looked down at his plate.

"Please God, tell me I got the malaria and fever's making all of this seem real," he muttered. "Tell me I ain't here but home in Georgia."

The Pinkertons came through the door and made their way to the back table. They spoke briefly to Serena and Galloway, then went outside.

"Holt talked to them two fellows yesterday," Snipes said. "They was down there in Brazil awhile. Said that jungle's full of awful critters. If it swims or flies or crawls it's out to kill you."

"Sounds like all they'd lacked was a Galloway," Henryson said.

"They got one now," Snipes said, "and I wish they'd kept him."

The bell clanged and the men gulped down their coffee and gathered in the still-dark yard. The Pinkertons handed each of the dozen foremen a box of matches and a thick three-foot branch of hickory swabbed in pitch.

"This ain't light enough for us to work by," a foreman named Wells complained.

"But you'll be up there ready when there is light enough," a Pinkerton answered.

"Without our watches when will we know it's time to break or eat?" another foreman asked.

"The bell will tell you all you need to know," the other Pinkerton answered.

Matches flared and the pitch caught. First light smudged the eastern sky as the torches made a widening constellation across the valley floor. When the crews arrived where yesterday's work had ceased, the trees began emerging from the dark.

"Damn if she didn't cipher it to the minute," Snipes said, snuffing out the torch.

Yesterday, Snipes and Henryson had felled a sugar maple and a white oak, clearing space to begin sawing one of the largest trees in the valley, a chestnut so wide three men could not have linked arms around it. Henryson stared at the tree and shook his head.

"I get blisters just looking at that thing."

"It is right sizable, but it's dying of the blight," Snipes said, pointing to an orange fungus on the bark, "which makes me feel a bit less bad to cut it. There was some winters chestnuts was near all that kept me and my family's bellies filled."

As the men began to saw and chop, gray clouds settled over the valley. Serena loosed the eagle again and men paused to watch it circle the valley twice before bolting downward to scuffle briefly, then arise with another rattlesnake.

"That's the fearsomest bird I ever seen," Quince said.

The men resumed work. Trees began to fall. Some could hardly be heard, the sound little more than the thrash and scrape of sheared limbs. But the bigger trees, the oaks and poplars and hickories, made the whole ridge shake. After what seemed three hours, the loggers listened in vain for the bell to signal the midmorning break. Ross notched a few more trees, then chopped down a stand of smaller blackjack oaks as Quince continued to limb.

Close by, Henryson and Snipes kept sawing the chestnut. Sawdust sifted the two men's clothing and skin like pollen. Ross helped too, placing the blocks and steel wedges each time the crosscut saw pinched. They were now in the trunk's heart and the saw's rasps slowed. The men paused and wiped their brows and, still on their knees, placed hands on their backs and stretched.

"I used to wonder why old-timers called that thing a misery whip," Henryson said, nodding at the saw, "but I know now."

Once through the core, the sawing was easier. The gap widened and more wedges were needed. The great tree began to tremble, its branches grasping at the sky as if seeking purchase. Snipes yelled "timber" and the men scattered. The upper branches crackled and snapped against other trees. Brown leaves gusted as a squirrel's nest burst. The ground quaked as the chestnut hit, causing every crew on the ridge to pause.

As the men rested, Snipes looked at the sky and nodded to himself in grim satisfaction. The other men waited for some pronouncement but none came. The men gazed longingly up the ridge where their lunch buckets awaited them. Gray clouds thickened over the valley, yet no rain fell.

"I figured she might cut our morning break," Quince said, "but ain't she gonna give us time to eat?"

Henryson had a finger on the chestnut's stump, his lips moving as he counted aloud.

"I count two hundred and thirty-seven rings," he said. "I doubt there's one older in this valley."

"If you're talking about trees and not that hag," Snipes said.

He and Henryson began sawing a white ash as Ross helped Quince limb the chestnut. As the crews around them worked on, mishaps occurred. The injured loggers had to be helped across the valley floor to the blue boxcar.

One was carried straight to the graveyard. The crew next to Snipes's stumbled off the ridge, swatting and swearing as hornets swarmed around them. One man rolled on the ground as if on fire, while another wallowed facedown in the silt-clogged creek.

When the bell finally rang, the crew stuffed food into their mouths so quickly that they barely chewed. Beef jerky usually saved for the midafternoon break was devoured too.

"Lord, I wish that chestnut was alive," Henryson said when they'd finished. "I'd eat them nuts, green shells and all."

"Me too," Quince said, taking out his tobacco pouch and rolling papers.

Snipes lit his pipe and paused to study the sky again.

"I think they've went and done it," he said.

"Done what?" Henryson asked.

"What that Einstein fellow in Switzerland's argued," Snipes said.

"Which is?"

"He claims you can stretch time out like it was taffy."

"Where'd you hear such bullshit as that, Snipes?" Henryson asked.

"He's even got the formula to prove it."

Henryson looked over at his cousin.

"You ever hear a thing like that at college?"

Ross shook his head.

"It did seem near forever before the lunch bell rang," Quince said uneasily.

"I never even heard it being tried," Henryson said.

Snipes took a long draw on his briar pipe, slowly let the smoke purl out.

"If you was to try and didn't want for anyone excepting you to know," Snipes said, "what'd be the first thing you would do?"

"Get rid of all the clocks and watches," Quince said, his voice draining to a whisper.

"But there's one other way to tell the time," Snipes said.

Henryson looked heavenward, but no sun shone through the clouds.

"Them clouds will move on soon enough," Henryson said.

"We'll see about that," Snipes said.

Henryson turned to Ross.

"Tell me this don't make a lick of sense."

"If anyone could do it," Ross answered, "they'd be the ones."

The bell clanged again only as the day's last gray light expired. The torches were relit and the men made their descent. Foremen wove around the stumps and slash, their crews close behind. From a distance, flames streamed down the ridge as if molten. Some workers tripped, tumbling downhill like ballhooted logs. Quince banged his shin on a stump and bumped Henryson. Both men fell, their lunch buckets clattering to the valley floor. When the torches reached level land, their flames came together as if funneling back into their initial source.

Once at camp, the foremen gathered around a hoop barrel filled with water. The torches smoked and hissed as they were doused. As Snipes's crew went into the mess hall, they passed the photograph of Rachel Harmon, Galloway's knife still embedded in her throat.

Another cook and extra servers had been hired, and as the men sat down, food already steamed on the tables before them: platters piled with bloody steaks and fried chicken, yellowware brimming with corn and potatoes, baskets of cornbread and butter-drenched biscuits. Coffee too, not in the usual containers with spouts but five-gallon pots men dipped cups into as they might soup or cider. Servers whisked away dishes with the same speed as in the morning, but even with a head start, the men ate so fast that the servers barely kept up. Taste preferences deferred to whatever was most easily reached. Some loggers dispensed with cutlery, ate hand to mouth. More food came, seemingly taken from larders at random, field peas and pickles, rice, beets, and cheese. Then more biscuits, set beside them tins of jam and honey and molasses. Snipes's crew emptied their table's containers three times before they were sated enough to speak.

"I never eat so much in all my life," Henryson said when he finally set down his knife and fork.

"Stoking us like we're nothing but machines," Ross said.

Loggers around them suddenly grew quieter, many looking at the main door. Snipes's crew turned to see Sheriff Bowden, hat held belt-high before him, waiting to be noticed. His lips were pinched tight, evoking not so much stoicism as resignation. Serena nodded and he walked to the back table and began conversing with her. When they'd finished talking, Galloway banged a wooden salt shaker gavel-like on the table. Bowden turned and faced the loggers. He cleared his throat and spoke.

"We are still searching for Rachel Harmon, so any information about her possible whereabouts is needed. Also, William Meeks's body was found in the Tuckasegee River this afternoon. We haven't the least cause to suspect his death to be anything other than an accidental drowning."

Bowden turned, nodded at Serena, and quickly walked past the tables and out the door.

"Sheriff Bowden didn't seem to notice that Galloway's suspenders are the ones that he saw Meeks wearing just last night," Henryson said.

"Justice is blind," Snipes said, "includes color-blind too."

"Despite them suspenders, I was holding out a bit of hope that Meeks just up and left," Quince said. "He warn't the worst boss ever I worked for."

"Don't seem they've struck trail on that Harmon girl," Henryson said. "Maybe she's going to dodge them after all."

The loggers began to rise from the tables and go outside. Soon Snipes's crew joined them as they gathered around the porch steps.

Snipes spotted Murrell talking with two foremen.

"I think I'll go and hear the scuttlebutt," Snipes said.

Most loggers were already heading to the bunkhouse to sleep.

"Them fellows yonder has the right idea," Quince said, and followed them.

"I had a mind to play some rook or checkers, but I'm too tuckered out," Henryson said to Ross. "What about you, cousin?"

Before Ross could answer, the loggers around them began clearing a path below the steps. One of the men caught Henryson's eye and nodded at the porch. Galloway and his mother, linked elbow to elbow in a manner almost matrimonial, were coming out the mess hall door.

Henryson tugged his kinsman's sleeve and took a step backward, but Ross remained where he was, not directly in their path, but close enough that Galloway would have to lead his mother around him.

"Get out of our way, Ross," Galloway said when he and his mother neared the bottom step.

Ross didn't move. Galloway and his mother stopped.

"I'm going to have to take the shine off you," Galloway said. "Take more than that if I have a mind to."

"You can't take a thing I care about," Ross replied.

Galloway placed his thumb and index finger on one of the purple suspenders, looked down as if inspecting the material for some stain or flaw.

"They's many a man that would disagree," Galloway said, his eyes slowly rising from the cloth. "Of course, they ain't around to tell you."

"I said anything I care about," Ross answered.

Galloway's mother tugged at her son's arm.

"I got a couple of others to take care of first," Galloway said as he brushed past Ross, "but our time will come."

As Galloway and his mother slowly made their way to the farmhouse, Henryson placed his hand on his kinsman's elbow.

"Come on," Henryson said, urging Ross toward the bunkhouse.

*The broad-winged hawk left, many in pairs, others*
*singly, then the carolina parakeet and yellow-billed cuckoo,*
*barred owl and indigo bunting, and then the cedar waxwing*
*and wild turkey, wood thrush and scarlet tanager, ruffed*
*grouse and northern cardinal, and after that the yellow*
*warbler and goldfinch, barn swallow and rose-breasted*
*grosbeak, red-winged blackbird and eastern bluebird, raven*
*and mourning dove . . .*

# 8

He had thought that she was talking in her sleep, but then, as he was about to undress, Galloway realized that his mother was awake. He listened to what she said and went downstairs. Serena was speaking to the Pinkertons about tomorrow. He glared at the men. They could strut around with their shiny badges and bowler hats, shave every day and dab perfume on afterward, but to his way of thinking, there wasn't nothing that made shit smell sweet.

"We got need to talk," Galloway said to Serena. "Just us."

Serena nodded and the Pinkertons left.

"What is it?"

"Momma says we're too far away to hone in on that gal," Galloway said, "so me and her need to get on the train come morning."

"You know I need you both here to make the deadline," Serena said. "Leave on Saturday. I'll return to Brazil as we planned. You two stay until it's done."

Galloway remembered the rainy morning when this woman had saved his life. She had tied the tourniquet above his severed limb, helped him onto the Arabian. Serena had gripped the reins with one hand, the other arm wrapped around his waist, pressing Galloway's smaller body against hers as they galloped back to the camp. He would be bound to her for life, that was part of his mother's prophecy, as was their dying together. Each now bound to the other.

"Momma said if we don't find that child soon, there'll be a time when that child finds us."

For a few moments Serena didn't speak.

"*Soon*, that's all she said, nothing about how soon."

"Yes."

"Then we'll get enough trees down tomorrow. You'll leave Friday morning, maybe even Thursday night. Twelve hours, twenty-four at most, that's soon enough."

Galloway went back up the stairs. He stood by the bed and waited, but his mother did not speak again so he undressed and went to bed.

The window was open. The relative quietness made him yearn for Brazil even more. He missed the sounds of the jungle's night stalkers, the screeches and snarls as they attacked each other. It was the most honest place he knew. From the very start you knew near everything was out to kill you. Vines would snag and hang a man, and the forest was so thick you could wander off a few yards and never be seen again. In the Amazon things came straight at you. Bats big as turkeys dropped from the sky to suck your blood, jaguars leaped out of trees to rip your throat out. Underfoot were bushmasters that made rattlers look like garter snakes and there were fer-de-lances that could kill a full-grown man in five minutes. Even the bright-colored frogs oozed with poison. The water was even worse. There were fish that swarmed on you like hornets and whittled you down to your bones, and eels that could shock you, and stingrays and catfish with poison in their tails and fins, and even a little-bitty fish that swam right up your pecker and got you that way. There were caimans and anacondas and the water itself was black as tar so you couldn't see nothing till it grabbed hold of you. No, in the Amazon you didn't need a nickel to go in some tent. It was all free and out in the open with nary a trapdoor to cheat folks.

The nub began to ache and he rubbed it. *Soon.*

# 9

Even on those first mornings as he watched older students go to the board with chalk, it was the numbers, not the letters, that captivated him. He loved how numbers didn't change. Grammar and spelling always had exceptions: you *are,* not *is. I* before *e* except after *c.* But added or subtracted, multiplied or divided, the numbers worked the same. Though he could not articulate it then, he believed he'd found a way to understand the world.

Soon he was so far beyond the others that Miss Jenkins got him textbooks from the junior high, then the high school. In algebra, letters returned, but now they were consistent. At the end of seventh grade, Miss Jenkins presented him with a slide rule and a manual that taught him how to use it. He learned how to gauge the weight of water as gallons, the horsepower of a waterfall, to alter gears on a lathe. All he had to do was move the slide a few inches and the answer would appear. There was a beauty in it, because the numbers were always true.

*Your son is so bright. It would be a shame for him not to continue his education.*

His parents had been reluctant, but he'd promised to

complete his chores, do farm work all day Saturday. So they
allowed him to ride horseback five miles to Waynesville
High School, where he won the math award two years
straight. Mr. Randolph, the principal, helped him get a
work scholarship at the college in Cullowhee, promising
that a teaching job would be waiting when he received his
degree. By then he'd begun to spend Sunday evenings with
Emma Parton, who lived on the adjoining farm. Before he
left for college they announced their engagement. Their
parents promised a wedding gift of ten acres between the
two farms. He and Emma picked out the place on the land
where they'd build their house and make a home.

At the college, he learned about Pythagoras, who gave
him words for what he had felt, that math and reality were
indeed one thing. His teachers urged him to go on to a university, perhaps one day discover theorems of his own, but
that was not in the plan. He'd gotten his teaching certifi-
cate and taken a job at Waynesville High School. He and
Emma married two weeks after his graduation.

Each morning he rode back and forth on horseback, though
sometimes foul weather or late school events forced him to stay
in town overnight. He taught grades eight and nine, awaiting
the moments when the students' eyes brightened with under-
standing. On weekends he began building his own house. He
went to the lumberyard with only a mathematical calculation
on a single piece of paper:

$$40^2 + 30^2 = c^2$$
$$1600 + 900 = 2500$$
$$C = \sqrt{2500}$$
$$C = 50$$

He calculated the sawn lumber for the subfloor and dressed lumber for the main floor so there would not be a single shim needed. A 12-and-12-inch run for the pitch of the roof so that every cut would be at 45 degrees. Then calculations for gutters and shingles, even the number of nails. On weekends men, including those from the lumberyard, came to watch the house rise, believing experience trumped the veracity of numbers. His father and father-in-law helped, though skeptical at times themselves. But the house rose exactly as the numbers said it would, as if the wood and metal merely confirmed what had always been there. When the last nail had been driven into the last shingle, no man could find fault. For the next six years he taught at the high school. A daughter was born, then a second. Money was saved to purchase an automobile.

Their children were five and two when influenza ravaged the county. Brought back by soldiers, some claimed. One of his students died; another lost her father. He'd been terrified he would bring the contagion home, but then the epidemic waned. No new outbreaks for weeks. On a spring Saturday the family went to Waynesville. The next night Susie came down with a fever. He had taken the thermometer from the medicine cabinet and set it in her mouth. 100.2. He checked it again the next morning. 98.6. Emma suggested he have the doctor come from Waynesville, but the number reassured him. There was a PTA meeting on Monday evening, and he did not get home until after ten. By then Susie was delirious and Emma and Mae had taken to bed. By the time he got the doctor, it was too late. His family was nothing more than three filled coffins.

The principal told him to take two weeks off, a month

if needed. They could take care of his classes. But he turned in his resignation. He refused his neighbors' help and dug the graves alone. In labor he found what no words from preacher, friend, or kin could give him. After hours of flinging dirt at the sky, he exhausted himself into numbness. It wasn't anything like peace or acceptance, but it allowed him a few hours of oblivion. So he sold the land and house and sought such work elsewhere, but not before buying stones to mark the graves. He bought a fourth stone and set it beside the others for the time when the misery would end and he'd join them.

At the Sunburst logging camp, they offered him a job as a bookkeeper, but he was finished with numbers so asked for an ax instead. Then he'd moved on to work for the Pembertons. For twelve years, he'd never allowed himself to care about what happened to him or to anyone else. But had his eldest daughter lived, she and Rachel Harmon would have been almost the same age. Last fall, when the girl and child were hiding in Kingsport, the crone had found her. And now she might again, and this time they would not escape.

As Ross lay on his cot among the other loggers, he wondered if he had been wrong again: that, unlike him, Galloway, Galloway's mother, and Serena Pemberton had found a theorem that *could* take the measure of the world, a theorem they'd further validate by cutting the throats of an eighteen-year-old girl and her child.

Ross fell asleep and dreamed of a fourth grave finally filled.

# 10

The next morning the loggers ate fiercely. There were pancakes and eggs, biscuits and grits and gravy, but also beef and ham and chicken. Coffee was again in five-gallon pots set on each table. The men, many exhausted from the day before, dipped out cup after cup. More baskets of biscuits came. When the molasses and honey ran out, jars of jam were brought, their colors and containers so varied it was clear root cellars all over the county had contributed, though by force or barter no logger knew.

"It's like I got a big hole in my belly and food runs out quick as I can swallow," Henryson said, grabbing another biscuit.

When the work bell rang, men stuffed their overall pockets with biscuits, placed as many in their lunch pails as would fit, and went outside.

As Snipes's crew came down the mess hall steps, a light rain began falling.

"Like that ridge warn't slick enough already," Quince said.

"At least you've got some brightness on today," Snipes said, eyeing Quince's red shirt and yellow kerchief.

As the foremen lit their torches, Serena appeared on horseback. Following behind her were two dozen men never seen before. Some were young, others gray-haired and grizzled. Their lack of scars and nubbed fingers made clear none were experienced loggers. As did their ragged, denimless attire: madras and cassimere pants, poplin and broadcloth shirts. Some wore scuffed oxfords or wingtips instead of boots. All carried shiny new axes in their hands.

"On this morning we'll all go out together," Serena said.

The Pinkertons led, railroad lanterns in hand. Serena and Galloway came next, then the regular crews, torches aloft. The new men came last, their faces wary. The procession made its way to the left base of the uncut ridge and halted. As one crew ascended, Serena took twenty strides to the right and signaled the next up the flank. When half the veteran crews had peeled off, she tripled the number of footsteps and summoned the new recruits.

"Any tree that you can't link your arms around," Serena said, "leave for the sawyers."

"How far up do we go?" a thin man in a white pongee shirt asked.

"Until you tumble down the yonder side," Galloway said. "And one more thing. You best not be lolling when we come round."

Serena took another thirty paces and Snipes's crew made its ascent.

"Them's the sorriest bunch of wood hicks I ever seen," Henryson said when they reached where trees replaced stumps. "Where'd they get them fellows, anyway?"

"Bowden found them in the hobo camps," Snipes

answered. "Charged the lot with vagrancy and sentenced them to three days working here. Murrell said they'll likely bring in more."

The sound of axes began in the ridge's center, but the veteran crews tarried.

"I'm worn plumb out and yet to saw a lick," Henryson said.

"Even with my eyes shut I see trees," Quince said. "I dreamed all night that I was cutting them."

"Sure it was a dream?" Snipes said.

"Don't start with that stuff, Snipes," Henryson said. "We got a pharaoh's plague of troubles now that we're awake."

"Sure that we're awake?" Snipes asked.

Exasperated, Henryson turned to Ross.

"Can't you show the nonsense of his notions?"

"All I know is I want it to end," Ross said.

A cry followed by a moan came from their left.

"Bowden better find her some more men," Henryson said. "Them over there is gonna thin out quick."

Snipes went up the ridge, stopped in front of a hickory to judge its girth. As he did, an ax came twirling toward him. With a loud thwack the blade entered the bark just above Snipes's cap and bells.

"Shit fire!" Quince cried out. "Ain't there enough to put us in a grave without our having axes hove our way?"

Snipes reached up and pulled the ax free, examined it as he might some rare artifact.

"I venture it the first tree that ax hit," Henryson said.

A man in a striped broadcloth shirt appeared out of the fog. Unlike the soiled pants, the shirt looked newly washed, leading Snipes to suspect it had been snatched off a clothesline.

"You looking for this?" Snipes asked.

"Yeah," the man answered.

"You ever logged before?" Snipes asked.

"Well, no," the man answered, "but I'll soon catch the hang of it."

"Let me offer you a suggestion," Snipes said, handing the man the ax. "It works a whole lot better if you hold on when you swing instead of throwing it."

The man disappeared back into the fog.

"I'd say it's best to get on back to work," Snipes said. "A moving target's always harder to hit."

The men picked up their tools and began to work. Not long after, cooks and servers came up the ridge carrying pails of water, leaving two with each crew before heading back to camp.

"Whatever that's about, it ain't good," Henryson said.

The rain ceased, but the sun did not appear. Instead, tendrils of fog began to knit together. The fog covered the valley floor and, like water filling a pond, slowly rose. The camp buildings disappeared, then the ridges. The fog seemed to have swaddled the world inside some older measure. What had been cracks sharp as gunshots were now not only softened but also unsourced. In some places, such was the denseness that ax heads floated into view, vanished before striking wood. Logs hooked to cables appeared too late to be dodged. Crews lost all bearings of where other crews were. The injured were hard to locate, and their muffled cries and moans filled the ridge. More trees fell, but how far or near was hard to gauge, as some men realized too late.

A neighboring logger yelled "hornets." Men rushed toward Snipes's crew waving their hats wildly as cowboys caught in a cattle stampede. Snipes's crew was soon swatting at the insects too, incurring their own stings before the hornets retreated. When the hickory Snipes and Henryson sawed fell, Henryson gave an exhausted sigh.

"Ain't no wood in Brazil any harder to saw than locust and hickory," he said.

"I'd not argue it," Snipes said, "but there's a tree you'll be glad to see."

Snipes pointed up the ridge where the fog had begun to lighten. Just visible through the mist, a smidge of green appeared amid the hardwood trunks.

"Please tell me that ain't just some rhododendron," Henryson said.

"It's a fir," Snipes said. "We're getting near the top."

All the while, Serena and Galloway made their rounds, the horse's coat so closely matching the fog that Serena at first appeared to hover above the ground. Galloway trod on foot, but with such soundlessness that men found him suddenly there. Twice Serena and Galloway came upon men asleep. The henchman's steel-capped boot kicked them awake as Serena told them they were fired. Each tumbled down the ridge, Galloway still kicking at ribs already cracked. The Pinkertons patrolled the ridge too, blackjacks in hand, and dealt similar punishments.

Serena and Galloway passed by Snipes's crew but did not linger, though Galloway and Ross exchanged glares. Not long after, an ashen-faced logger came out of the fog, a gash in his upper leg spurting blood. He did not pause for aid or solace, but staggered past the crew and tumbled down the ridge and out of sight. Wounded men continued to call out from the fog.

"My stomach argues that it's way past noon," Quince complained, and Henryson quickly agreed.

Snipes declared a brief break. The men ate the biscuits stuffed in their overalls, washed them down with water from the pails.

"My Lord, just listen to them poor souls," Quince said. "How can you help a man who can't be found? I never seen such fog in all my days."

"Best be glad you got some color on you," Snipes said. "It gives a bit more visioning amongst us."

"What you said last night about the weather," Quince said to Snipes. "You meant this here fog, didn't you?"

"It or something else to hide the sun."

"You think that hag is down there in this mess?" Henryson asked.

"Not to conjure where that girl and child are," Snipes said, "but this weather argues that she's keeping herself busy."

Ross had picked up his ax, but suddenly turned.

"Why do you say that, Snipes?"

"Murrell said the girl's so far away that witch can't get her beaded good."

"It's not like them to give up," Ross said.

"They're not," Snipes said. "Galloway and the hag are heading west."

"When?"

"Either late tonight or in the morning."

"By train?" Ross asked.

Snipes nodded and the men returned to work.

The fog began to lighten, not only above but around the men, enough so that several injured loggers were found and helped across the valley to the boxcar. More trees fell, were hooked to cables, then, as if adrift some current, floated above the valley floor to where the loader and flatcars waited. The soil became thinner and the trees smaller and farther apart. As Snipes and Henryson sawed a sixty-foot chestnut oak, Ross moved above to clear a patch of mountain holly. Snipes yelled "timber" and the oak teetered. More trees remained to be sawed, but a gap the width of a Biltmore stick opened upward before them, allowing the first view of the rock-domed crest.

## 11

When Jacob was a week old, Rachel had set the child on the ground to feel the rocky Appalachian soil, to begin to know his place in the world. She'd taken him around the farm to touch the trees and wildflowers, the furrows where the land was plowed. She'd placed the child's hand firm to the earth. *Feel of it,* she'd told Jacob, *this is your home.* Despite all the hardships change had brought, especially her father's death, Rachel had found comfort knowing the surrounding mountains were steadfast, could even believe that they would watch over her and Jacob.

But North Carolina was no longer home for Jacob, so one Sunday Rachel took him to where the Duwamish River flowed into the ocean. They followed a trail to the Pacific shore. Rachel immersed Jacob's hand in the water, raised his fingers to his lips so he might taste the ocean brine. She let him crawl around and sink his hand into the sand, feel seaweed and rocks and shells. *This is our home now,* Rachel told him. She too tasted the water.

Rachel finished dressing for work, quickly changed Jacob's hippin. The black-sailed ship had come again last night, except Galloway wasn't alone. Beside him stood a tiny woman, her face concealed inside a black bonnet. She remembered the morning when Miss Stephens had shown her third-grade class a map of the United States. She'd pointed out North Carolina, then asked Joel Vaughn to come up and point out the farthest place away. Joel had looked at the map a few moments and put his finger on a dot that had *Seattle* above it.

Where else could she and Jacob flee, if they were already as far away as possible? Rachel thought of the thousands of miles she and Jacob had traveled, all of the towns and cities where she could have decided *This is far enough* but always going farther. If Galloway could find them here, a whole continent away, he could find them anywhere. No, Rachel decided. They would not run again. She placed the bowie knife in the long right pocket of her work skirt. She lifted Jacob. *Seattle,* she told him. *This is our home.*

# 12

*It's better if you handle this alone. As I have said before, her partners tend to live much longer when they keep their distance, and that includes a matter such as this.*

These were Calhoun's words an hour earlier, after reminding Brandonkamp it was he who'd altered the contract. As if Brandonkamp needed reminding, hadn't spent hours thinking about anything else. *All equipment must be loaded on train cars by the deadline.* The sentence, each word, each syllable, wailed inside his head like a banshee. Lawyer Weatherbee cautioned him not to make the change. It's not worth it, the amount of money you gain is so minimal, the lawyer had told him. Why hadn't he listened to Weatherbee and Calhoun, the others who'd dealt with this she-devil? He'd even bragged about besting Serena Pemberton at the Grove Park, then ordered sherry and cigars for all. Only then, glasses filled and cigars lit, did Calhoun (of course it would be Calhoun) ever so casually mention Meeks's drowning. *Obviously nothing more than a tragic accident,* Calhoun had noted dryly. *Probably just out for his constitutional, chose to stroll along the riverbank and fell in. He did walk two miles to get to that riverbank and did so in the middle of the night, but we all have our quirks. Nothing about it suspicious at all,* Calhoun had concluded, and raised his glass to Brandonkamp. *Cheers.*

Brandonkamp left the blacktop and began his descent into the valley. He was dressed in his best business suit, dark tie to better show his gold tie clasp, a reminder that, unlike Meeks, he was a man of some importance. Unfortunately, the Packard had been built for a real road, not a goat trail, and its size made the descent more dangerous. Another thought came: the maniac Galloway driving from the other direction. At any moment his face might appear behind the Pierce-Arrow's steering wheel, the highlander still smoking his infernal cigarette as he calmly awaited the collision that would send both automobiles into the abyss.

Brandonkamp squinted his eyes, hoping to see better, but it did not help. He'd expected Meeks to be chastised for his lack of business acumen, perhaps even fired, but killed? He'd protested as much to Calhoun, who responded with gleefully unnerving accounts of others around Mrs. Pemberton who'd suffered similar "misfortunes," a litany of hunting mishaps, falls down stairs, and automobile wrecks, aside from shootings and stabbings. When Brandonkamp asked for at least some small piece of advice, Calhoun suggested a life jacket.

The fog shrouding the road made his journey even more treacherous. The Packard now moved at a funereal pace. And he dark-suited as a mourner. Brandonkamp wished he'd stayed out of the timber business and continued to work on Wall Street. In New York, people at least behaved in a civilized manner when they made fortunes fleecing others. But no, at forty-eight, he had to strike out to build a timber empire, and, irony of ironies, one inspired by George Pemberton's success. He drove even slower, twice having to stop and get out, ensure there was a road and not a drop-off before him.

The ground finally leveled and he passed the mess hall and farmhouse. When he pulled up in front of the office, Galloway stood on the steps as if expecting him. Brandonkamp did not exit the Packard immediately. Instead, he gripped the steering wheel so hard his hands reddened. He had always been good at negotiations, he reminded himself and at Princeton, an orator of some note. He tilted his head to catch his reflection in the mirror. Wishing to see something other than a fool, he fixed his gaze on the manly chin and thick mustache. Even the gray hair was a reminder he'd been a businessman, a very successful one, longer than Serena Pemberton had been alive. Brandonkamp straightened his shoulders and got out of the car. He looked toward the east ridge. It was immersed in whiteness. Most everything else was as well. Work continued. He could hear the shay engine, the skidder and McGiffert loader. Such conditions surely slowed the progress, though that hardly mattered now.

"I need to speak to Mrs. Pemberton," Brandonkamp said.

Galloway appeared to ponder the request, then nodded. The door was open so Brandonkamp went in. Galloway followed, shutting the door behind him. Serena closed a ledger and stood. To emphasize her superior height, Brandonkamp suspected.

"What brings you here today, Brandonkamp?" Serena said tersely. "Another proviso?"

"Certainly not," Brandonkamp stammered. "As a matter of fact, getting rid of the one in the contract is the main reason why I am here."

"And the other reason?"

Brandonkamp's smile widened as if a bit had been inserted. Why in God's name hadn't he just said *the* and left out *main*. Meeks's death was not to be brought up until later, after goodwill and trust had been established, not in his opening gambit.

"Hardly important at all," Brandonkamp answered, waving a dismissive hand for emphasis. "Much more important is the contract, which I've given much thought to, and recognize . . ."

"But first the other reason for your coming," Serena said. "It's better to have all matters addressed from the start."

Brandonkamp thought of making up another reason, but with her gray eyes staring right into his, she'd know it was a lie, and that would only make things worse.

"Well, Calhoun mentioned to me the death of Mr. Meeks."

"What of it?" Serena said, her tone not defensive but casual.

"The suddenness I find, well, troubling, especially since he was the one who agreed to the proviso."

"So you believe they are connected, is that what you're saying?"

"It's just . . ."

"If you believe it is something more than coincidence, not an accident but foul play," Serena said, "you should go to Sheriff Bowden's office. Perhaps you even have suspects?"

"No, nothing of the sort, Mrs. Pemberton. I'm just saying . . ."

"You ain't said much of nothing yet," Galloway sneered.

Without the garrulous Calhoun present, the office should have felt larger, but with each exchange the walls seemed to close in, drawing the three of them closer and closer. He contemplated sitting down, but that would only make him feel smaller, more vulnerable. Brandonkamp thought hard for the right words, the right order. Then he found them, what he should have said at the very start.

"The reason I came, the whole reason, is my sincere wish to conclude our negotiations on the best of terms."

"What are you suggesting?"

For the first time since entering the room, Brandonkamp heard a tone that, while not conciliatory, wasn't outright hostile.

"That we forget this nonsense of a proviso, Mrs. Pemberton. I'll pay your original asking price without the ten percent penalty regarding the equipment. Glad to do so, actually. It was, after all, rather unfair of me. I see that now and wish to make amends."

"Amends?"

"Yes," Brandonkamp said. "I prefer we part on the best of terms."

Serena looked out the window, though with the omnipresent fog, there was nothing to see. Galloway struck a match, but it seemed done with some delicacy, as if not to disturb his master's concentration. Though Brandonkamp watched intently, nothing in her demeanor changed, but her left hand, almost invitingly, gestured at the chair beside her.

"Mahogany," Serena said. "I know there's still profit to be made here, but in another year, two years at most, all the inexpensive tracts will be bought up. The future is Brazil, though there are risks in such a venture, which others in our business are too timid to take. But I've never been afraid of risk, have you?"

*No,* Brandonkamp was about to say, but checked himself.

"Why do you ask, Mrs. Pemberton?"

"I have a better way to part, as you suggest, on the best of terms."

"Which is?"

"We wager, all or none," Serena said. "If I miss the Friday deadline, the equipment is yours for free, but if I make the deadline, you pay me double." She took out a piece of paper, wrote on it, and slid it across the table. "Whether I win or lose, I assure you that we'll part on the best of terms."

He stared at the paper as he might a treasure map afloat in quicksand.

"But with all due respect, you will surely lose."

Brandonkamp's mind teetered. He was certain the deadline could not be met. He'd seen the amount of uncut wood and the amount of men. He knew the machinery and what it could do and how quickly. He even knew, as Calhoun had assured him, that Serena Pemberton always honored business agreements. Yet another part of Brandonkamp warned, *Don't do it,* for somehow, somehow, this woman would find a way to make him lose. *But how?* It would have to be some sleight of hand, perhaps something she knew the fog would hide. What if they somehow made the road take him to a different valley, one already cleared? But even in the fog he'd seen all the buildings, heard the shay engine, the skidder and loader. As absurd as imagining that the ridge had simply floated into the ether.

But how could a man think clearly with her eyes boring into him and a knife-wielding golem at his back? Brandonkamp had a sudden urge to prevail.

"I need a minute to think this over, Mrs. Pemberton," Brandonkamp said, and stepped out on the porch.

He took a deep breath, let it out. The most primal directive of all came to him. If, against all logic, he lost, even if it nearly bankrupted him, at least he'd still be alive to write the check. But *would* he lose? Brandonkamp looked toward the east ridge. Still shrouded but, albeit faintly, he could hear the axes and saws. If he could just see the trees . . . But he had seen the trees, just two days ago, and knew at a glance that the deadline could not—would not—be met. And why couldn't Serena Pemberton be wrong? She'd run the business without George Pemberton for less than a year. What proof was there that her entire Brazil venture wasn't a boondoggle? All Calhoun had seen was a map.

Brandonkamp did a calculation of how many additional acres he could purchase, and felt his heart quicken. Definitely five hundred acres, perhaps five hundred and fifty if he could buy them right away, not in a year or two. He even knew the perfect tract in Macon County, for sale at this very moment. Brandonkamp looked toward the east ridge again. With his eight years' experience to less than one for her, how could he not know more? And yet . . .

Then Brandonkamp understood. The trick was so obvious that he'd nearly missed it.

"You were going to load the equipment and leave the remaining trees uncut," Brandonkamp said once back inside. "I must admit, Mrs. Pemberton, you almost had me. I would have made our wager, I promise you that, had I not realized your ruse."

"Then I take you at your word, Brandonkamp."

Serena opened up the desk drawer, took out the contract and a pen. She turned to the last page and added the information about all timber being cut and hauled away. She wrote her name and the date, pushed the contract to Brandonkamp's side of the desk.

He read the addendum twice. *Don't do it,* the voice in his head implored. But whose voice was that really—Calhoun's, the other gadabouts at the Grove Park? He still didn't pick up the pen.

"So you're not a man of your word, Brandonkamp?" Serena said, and nodded at his tie pin. "I would have expected more from a Princeton man."

He searched to find the right words, not for her but silently for himself. Distill it to one sentence he could truly, above all else, believe. And he did. *I know more about timber and deadlines than this woman.*

Brandonkamp picked up the pen and signed.

## 13

When the noon dinner bell finally rang, Snipes's crew devoured their food, then checked their pails and pockets for missed crumbs. Afterward, no one smoked and Snipes's newspaper went unread. Henryson and Quince sprawled out on the ground and began to snore. Snipes and Ross leaned against stumps and fell asleep also. The other crews apparently slept too, for silence fell over the ridge. Even the injured lost grew quieter, their low moans sounds any sleeper might make.

When the bell to resume work rang, Snipes yawned, rubbed his eyes, slapped his cheeks. He placed a blistered hand atop the stump that had been his pillow. Like a creaky accordion, Snipes's body didn't as much rise as unfold. Snipes roused the rest of the crew. As the others got to their feet, he stared down at the valley.

"Lord God," the foreman said.

"What is it, Snipes?" Henryson asked, standing beside him.

From the direction of the graveyard, human shapes emerged, but they did not walk like men. They approached, arms limp, gaits hesitant, like specters summoned from the deepest of sleeps. Fog unraveled around them like shroud cloth as they made their torpid progress across the valley floor. As they became more visible, Snipes and Henryson saw no chests or stomachs but skeletal alternations of slants and gaps. A clinking could be heard, as bones might make. When the figments ascended the ridge, the slants and gaps transformed into black and white stripes. Faces and shackles gained definition.

"I knowed it wasn't nothing but some jailbirds," Henryson said, but his voice trembled as he spoke.

The men went back to work. Parts of their bodies had begun to give out, altering movements. Henryson and Snipes switched sides mid-tree to rest shoulders. Quince's lower back had locked up, and he winced with each ax swing. Ross worked slower than anyone. After each chop, he lowered the ax blade to the ground, let it stay there while he deliberated the next strike. He no longer severed trees close to the ground, instead cut waist-high, the ax blade level as it entered the wood. The cut trees looked like fence posts. Yet each swing was delivered with precision and force, some trees felled with a single blow.

Snipes looked at Henryson.

"He's cutting high to provoke Galloway," Snipes said.

"You want me to try and talk to him?" Henryson asked.

"You think that he'd listen?"

"No, I don't."

"Then pray like hell that her and Galloway will be too busy with them new recruits," Snipes said. "Their next spat won't be words but blades and blood."

Whether time passed slow or fast, or even passed at all, Snipes and his men no longer knew, were uncertain even what day it was. The fog lightened but did not lift. Instead of time they had the ridgetop, which could be clearly seen now, though the men were so exhausted they feared that, as parched men in deserts saw oases before them, the crest might be a mirage. When Snipes's crew reached the first fir, Henryson rubbed the green needles, sniffed the clean, crisp scent.

"If we can smell it," he said, "then it must be real."

"Thirty yards and we'll be at the crest," Snipes said. "Just maybe we'll survive this after all."

Along the ridge, equally exhausted loggers suffered a litany of injuries. A bark chip blinded an eye, a severed branch speared a back, a cable hook cracked a skull. These men walked or were carried to the blue boxcar, where Watson ministered to them as best he could. A second wave of convicts came up the ridge. They did not shout "timber" or attempt to work together. They simply swung their axes until what stood before them fell.

Snipes's crew worked on. They were near somnolent now, tripping over stumps and slash, tangling their feet. Snipes and Henryson were out of sync, yanking each other's arms. Ross rested more between strokes. Quince's back was so painful that he could no longer bend. Instead of standing, he got down on hands and knees, gripping the ax like a hatchet as he chopped.

Quince was clearing away some shorn branches when he felt the bite. At first, he did not know what had happened. Then, looking closer, he saw the viper's slit eyes and triangular head. Quince jerked his hand away. The fangs remained clamped to Quince's wrist, and as he stumbled backward, the satin-black body lengthened to five feet before the blunt tail, vibrating fiercely, appeared. Still on the ground, Quince tried to shake the snake off, which caused the reptile to twine around the stricken limb.

"Get it off me," Quince screamed, and staggered to his feet.

He lifted the serpent-draped arm before him as if imploring both man and God. The reptile's mouth opened and struck again.

"Get it off me," Quince screamed again. He stumbled toward a tree and raked his forearm against it as if to peel the snake off.

"Hold still," Ross shouted, beside him now.

Ross finally stilled Quince enough to grab the snake behind its head, uncoil enough length that Snipes, pocket-knife out, could slash the body until the snake was ripped in two. Ross flung what part he held downridge. The rest, the rattle yet buzzing, slipped off Quince's arm and fell to the ground. Snipes turned Quince's forearm palm-up and grimaced.

"It got him in the vein," Snipes said. "Lean him against a stump and get that shirt off. Hurry."

As Henryson pulled off his belt and Snipes wiped the knife blade with his handkerchief, Ross kneeled beside Quince, placed his hands inside the shirt's collar, and jerked. Buttons flew off and Ross freed the shirt from the shoulder, then the arms and hands. Streaks of red already ran up the afflicted limb. An oily sweat covered Quince's face and arms and his body began to tremble.

"It's a dry bite, ain't it?" Quince asked, his voice quivering.

Henryson kneeled and looped his belt around the upper forearm.

"Higher, dammit," Snipes said. "This poison's moving fast."

Henryson slipped the belt higher, jerked it tight.

"It's a dry bite, ain't it?" Quince pleaded as the fore-man motioned for Ross to grip Quince's arm. "I wore the brightness."

Quince screamed and tried to jerk the arm free as Snipes cut an *X* across the first puncture, then the second. Snipes placed his mouth on the punctures, sucked and spit six times before wiping his mouth with his sleeve. The hand and forearm continued to swell.

"I got out all I could," Snipes said.

"You got to get it all," Quince moaned. "It's still too much inside me. I can taste the poison, Snipes. I swear I can."

"Tie it higher," Snipes said to Henryson, who loosened the belt, raised it to the armpit, and again jerked it tight. Snipes placed a hand on Quince's heaving chest.

"It's got to his heart," Snipes said.

"I wore the brightness, Snipes," Quince pleaded, sweat and tears mingling on his face. "Just like you said."

"I know you did," Snipes answered. "You done all you could."

Quince's whole body began to shake. A white foam gathered on his lips and his breaths began to shallow. Snipes leaned close and used finger and thumb to pull back an eyelid. The outer eye had begun to redden. He turned to Ross and Henryson.

"We got to try," Snipes said softly. "You go and I'll stay here. If I'm chopping they'll know we ain't asleep." Snipes turned back to Quince, placed a hand lightly on the stricken man's shoulder, and leaned close. "They're going to help you get down to the camp."

"My eyes is blurry," Quince said, each word an effort now, barely a whisper.

"They won't let you fall."

"Don't leave me in the fog."

"You know we won't," Snipes said and stood. "Move that arm little as you can," he told the two kinsmen, but though they did, Quince cried out before, mercifully, falling into unconsciousness.

By the time they got him to the boxcar, Quince's hand and arm had begun to blacken, his breath so shallow it was barely discernible. Bile and foam covered Quince's mouth and chin. His lips parted as if to speak, but no words came. Ross kneeled, took out a handkerchief, and wiped away the bile and foam. He balled up the handkerchief and closed Quince's unbitten hand around it. Watson had them set Quince on a pallet made of quilts. He examined the puncture marks and told them he'd do what he could.

Henryson and Ross began walking back. As they did, two loggers carrying a corpse came down the ridge.

"This has got to end," Ross said.

*The blue ridge salamander left first, then the pygmy salamander and red-backed salamander, then the long-tailed salamander and the marbled salamander, after them the fence lizard and five-lined skink, then spring peeper and box turtle, after that the unlimbed: black racer and green snake, garter snake and queen snake, water snake and king snake, copperhead and rattlesnake, corn snake and milk snake . . .*

# 14

As the last smudge of gray light was disappearing and the bell rang, Snipes and Henryson let go of the misery whip's handles. They left the blade midsaw inside a balsam's heartwood and got to their feet slowly, head down, one hand on the tree's trunk for support. Once upright, hands remained on the balsam as their necks unbent. When the dizziness subsided, Snipes lit the torch and he and Henryson picked up the lunch buckets, including Quince's. They joined Ross, who now stood beside the balsam, ax in hand.

"I ain't wanting to go down there yet," Henryson said. "Long as I'm up here I can believe he's still alive."

As the three men stood in silence, torches began winding down the ridge.

"We best get on moving," Ross finally sighed. "We'll lack the starch if we stay much longer."

Snipes's crew made their descent. On the valley floor they merged with the other loggers. In the glare of the torchlight, the loggers looked like casualties of a conflagration they'd yet to escape.

Some had bloody cloth or gauze wound around nubs

that had been fingers that morning. Others bore gashes and pumpknots. Men limped, some hopping on one foot while leaning on a comrade. Several loggers collapsed on the ground, one clutching his chest and expiring. *I got to sleep,* another said, waving his friends on.

As they entered camp, Snipes's crew veered toward the blue boxcar. The torch soon illuminated injured men lying on quilts. Among them stood Watson, wiping blood off his hands on an already bloody towel. When he saw Henryson and Ross, Watson shook his head, nodded toward the cemetery, where a grave was being filled.

"I had a bit of hope," Henryson said.

They watched until the grave was filled, a cross made of twine and two sawed hickory limbs planted at the head.

Snipes and Henryson began walking toward the mess hall, but Ross did not move.

"Come on, Ross," Snipes said.

"This ax needs sharpening," Ross answered.

"Take it to Mullins then," Snipes said. "We'll wait here."

"You all go on," Ross said, turned and left.

Henryson shrugged.

"I guess we may as well."

Snipes and Henryson went up the porch steps and entered the mess hall. They filled their plates, but as with so many of the loggers around them, they teetered between exhaustion and hunger. Some men ate awhile and then shut their eyes and leaned forward, resting foreheads on elbows before rousing themselves to eat more. All had to suppress yawns as they opened their mouths. Several men had crawled under the tables to sleep. Serena, Galloway, and Galloway's mother sat at the back table, paying little notice to the scene before them.

"I'll not survive another day like this," Henryson said.

"You won't have to," Snipes said. "We'll be finished by early afternoon."

"Sun time, or their time?"

"Sun time."

"We'll see," Henryson said skeptically, and glanced toward the door for a second time.

"What's taking him so long?" he said worriedly.

Just as he spoke, Ross entered, limping slightly as he approached the table. Henryson moved down the bench to make space, but Ross did not sit. Instead, he handed his kinsman a note, keeping the other arm and hand behind his back.

*Get me back home,* the note said.

"What do you mean by this?" Henryson asked, but Ross was already striding toward the back table. What he held behind his back was his ax.

Galloway rose, knife at the ready as Ross clambered onto the table, scattering dishes and platters as he gained his balance. After a moment's indecision, Galloway stepped to his right to protect Serena. He slashed at Ross's calves while loggers rushed for the door as the Pinkertons, revolvers drawn, shoved against the stampede. Ross leaped off the table and landed beside Galloway's mother. The crone was still seated when Ross pulled back the ax and paused, making a final calculation. Then the fresh-honed blade flashed toward her throat, entering just beneath her chin, slicing through the black bonnet's silk tie-string, then through skin and bone before the blade embedded itself in the wooden wall. Ross released the ax handle and stepped back. The men rushing toward the door froze, as did the Pinkertons. All watched as the crone's neck and shoulders sagged and, like a tent-show magic trick, her head appeared to levitate.

Two bullets entered Ross's back as Galloway's blade ripped open his stomach. Ross fell to the floor and the Pinkertons stood above him, still firing, filling the air with blue smoke and the odor of cordite. As the smoke drifted away, Galloway's mother reappeared. The bonnet had slipped off, revealing a pate hairless and pale except for a scrimshaw of purple veins. Then her body spasmed and folded over itself. The head remained where it had been, balanced on a blade bright as a silver platter.

# 15

As Rachel walked down the sidewalk, Jacob tucked dry beneath her slicker, she thought of Joel Vaughn. It was Joel, not Galloway or Galloway's mother, she'd dreamed of last night. In the dream Miss Stephens pointed out North Carolina on a map and asked Joel to find the safest place away from where they were, but before Joel chose, he asked Rachel to help him. So they'd pressed their palms together, index fingers touching as they pointed first north to Maine, then south to Texas, west to California before settling their fingertips on *Seattle*.

Rachel did not know if Joel was still alive, though shortly after arriving here, she'd thought she'd glimpsed him leaving the Salvation Army shelter, the same colored mackinaw he'd worn back at camp, red hair spilling out from under a black slouch hat. Wouldn't he think to flee here too? Or was that just wishful thinking? All she knew was what Sheriff McDowell had told her the night he drove Rachel to Tennessee: that Joel had saved her life. And this dream, surely it meant that she and Jacob would be safe here. Maybe, Rachel thought, it might mean even more.

# 16

The following morning the fog began dissipating, and by early afternoon the last wisps were gone. The clearing sky revealed dead men, some caught in attitudes that the living did not wish to contemplate. Two were impaled by sheared limbs, one had an ax imbedded in his skull, another had been decapitated by a snapped cable. A blackened arm reached out from under a slash pile, nearby a face masked by yellow jackets. In the cemetery below, men dug more graves.

On the east ridge's crest a single white pine rose mast-like above the valley's empty arc. Snipes and Henryson had already made their descent and loaded their tools into a boxcar. They watched the valley's last tree lean, casting a final shadow across the ridge. As the tree crashed to the ground, men loading equipment paused to watch as the sole crew left on the ridge quickly severed the branches and then, like harpooners, grasped iron peavey sticks to spear the shorn trunk. They prodded and shoved until the pine could be hooked to the last cable. For a few more moments, the only sounds were the rasp of shovels and splash of pitched dirt.

"When did Noah say we can get him took to Sylva?" Henryson asked Snipes.

"Soon as her and Galloway leave."

"He deserves more respect than being laid out inside a boxcar," Henryson said.

"Better than him still laying in that ditch," Snipes said. "We'll get him to Cataloochee in time to have him buried with his family by nightfall."

Henryson looked over at the graveyard.

"Quince won't even have that."

"I'll make sure Quince has at least a creek stone with his name," Snipes said. "A man ought not be totally forgotten."

An automobile could be heard coming toward the camp. A Packard Roadster came into view, rolled to a stop in front of the office. A gray-haired man got out. He stared at the east ridge and then at the train where the last equipment was being loaded onto a flatcar.

"That fellow looks a good bit out of sorts," Henryson said.

The man took out a pen and checkbook, walked into the office. He came out looking none the happier and drove away. Shortly afterward, Galloway left the building. He wore a black band on his right arm.

"What you reckon they done with the hag?"

"Holt said the undertaker come and got her," Snipes said, and gave a wan smile. "Whether the head or just the nigh end he didn't say."

"He hit her with a pretty lick for certain," Henryson mused.

"I'd like to think he took some pride in it," Snipes said, "even when he was laying there and dying."

"That Harmon girl and her child should be safe."

"Galloway's leaving, so I figure so," Snipes said.

With the last equipment loaded on the train cars, men began to line up in front of the office for their pay envelopes. Some sat in the dirt while they waited, too tired to stand. Others stood but with eyes closed. Galloway returned and went inside the office.

"So where will you be going after this?" Henryson asked.

"I think I'll farm if I can find some land that ain't been ruint," Snipes said, gazing at the wasteland around them. "Plant some apple trees, grow some beans and corn, taters and pumpkins too. If I can find a wife, I'll raise some kids to boot. What about you?"

"Up north to join the Wobblies," Henryson said. "No one else is making claim to helping poor folks like us."

Snipes looked toward the ridge and then the graveyard and shook his head.

"It's a wonder there's a one of us alive."

When the last man had been paid, Serena came out and gave some final instructions to Holt. Then she and the Pinkertons went into the barn. The Pinkertons came out first with the eagle's cage and placed it in the boxcar. Serena followed with the eagle on her arm. She spoke to Galloway, who walked over to the Pierce-Arrow and got in but didn't crank the engine. Serena did not take the eagle into the boxcar right away. Instead, she cast the bird and watched it circle the valley. Snipes and Henryson watched as well. Nothing on the ridges stirred. No squirrel chattered, no bird called, no tree rustled. Only silence. The eagle circled seven times before Serena blew the metal whistle and the bird returned. There was nothing left to destroy.

# Acknowledgments

Immense gratitude to Lee Boudreaux, Bette Alexander, Adam Eaglin, Tom Rash, Kathy Rash, Phil Moore, John Lane, Western Carolina University, Ann, Caroline, and James.

Ron Rash is the author of the PEN/Faulkner finalist and *New York Times* bestselling novel *Serena,* in addition to the critically acclaimed novels *The Risen, Above the Waterfall, The Cove, One Foot in Eden, Saints at the River,* and *The World Made Straight;* five collections of poems; and six collections of stories, among them *Burning Bright,* which won the 2010 Frank O'Connor International Short Story Award; *Nothing Gold Can Stay,* a *New York Times* bestseller; and *Chemistry and Other Stories,* which was a finalist for the 2007 PEN/Faulkner Award. Twice the recipient of the O. Henry Prize and winner of the 2019 Sidney Lanier Prize for Southern Literature, he is the Parris Distinguished Professor in Appalachian Cultural Studies at Western Carolina University.